Also by Mary McNear

Butternut Lake:

Also by Mary McNear

Butternut Summer
Up at Butternut Lake

Butternut Lake: The Night Before Christmas

MARY McNEAR

WILLIAM MORROW IMPULSE
An Imprint of HarperCollinsPublishers

17 July 24
B+T
3.99 (2.59)

This is a work of fiction. Names, characters, places, and incidents are products of the author's imagination or are used fictitiously and are not to be construed as real. Any resemblance to actual events, locales, organizations, or persons, living or dead, is entirely coincidental.

BUTTERNUT LAKE: THE NIGHT BEFORE CHRISTMAS. Copyright © 2015 by Mary McNear. Excerpt from *Moonlight on Butternut Lake* copyright © 2015 by Mary McNear. All rights reserved. Printed in the United States of America. No part of this book may be used or reproduced in any manner whatsoever without written permission except in the case of brief quotations embodied in critical articles and reviews. For information address HarperCollins Publishers, 195 Broadway, New York, NY 10007.

HarperCollins books may be purchased for educational, business, or sales promotional use. For information please e-mail the Special Markets Department at SPsales@harpercollins.com.

FIRST EDITION

Library of Congress Cataloging-in-Publication Data has been applied for.

ISBN 978-0-06-240681-1

16 17 18 19 OV/RRD 10 9 8 7 6

Chapter One

When Jack returned from bringing firewood in from the woodpile that night, he found Caroline standing in front of the mirror in their bedroom.

"What are you doing?" he asked, watching her from the doorway.

"What? Oh, nothing," she said, shaken out of her reverie and turning away from the mirror. "I was just, just checking something."

"Checking what?" Jack asked, coming over to her and taking her into his arms. She nestled against him and felt the cold night air, still on his flannel shirt and blue jeans, mix with the warmth of her white cotton nightgown.

"What were you checking on?" Jack persisted, nuzzling her neck in a way that almost made her forget what she'd been checking on. *Almost*. But she pulled away from him and showed him.

"Do you see this skin, right here, right under my chin?" she asked, patting it with her fingertips.

"I see it," he said. "And it looks beautiful," he added. "Like all of your skin."

"No, but I mean, feel it," she said. He felt it, dutifully. "Do you think it's getting a little softer? Do you think it's, you know, starting to *hang down* a little? You know, like the beginning of a double chin or a . . . a turkey wattle?"

"A turkey wattle?" Jack repeated, mystified.

Caroline nodded, seriously. "Because my grandma Pearl used to have this thing, this sack, sort of, that hung down under her chin, like a turkey wattle. At least that's what my cousins and I used to call it. And now I'm afraid I might be getting one too. I mean, not right this second, maybe, but at some point in the future."

"Caroline, there is nothing wrong with your chin, or the skin under your chin, or any other part of you, for that matter," he said, stroking her cheek tenderly. "Now what's this really about?"

"It's about aging, Jack," she said, a little fretfully. "It's about getting older."

"Something we're both going to do," he reminded her.

"Something we're both *already* doing," she said. "Only, because you're a man, you're doing it better than I am."

He studied her for a long moment. "So . . . is this about . . . are you thinking . . . that you're somehow going to be less attractive to me as you age?"

Caroline nodded, a little sheepishly. And then, before he could object, she said, "I know what you're going to say, Jack. And I already know all that stuff. 'It's what's on the inside that counts.' 'You'll love me whatever I look like. You're in this for the long haul' . . . all those things. And I get it. I believe you. It's just that . . . things are different with us. Our history is a little unusual." And that, they both knew, was putting it mildly. They'd married when they were both twenty-one and had their daughter, Daisy, soon after. Then they'd divorced three years later and had not seen each other again for the next eighteen years, until Jack had moved back to Butternut, Minnesota, last summer, still in love with Caroline, and hell-bent on winning her back. He had, eventually, and now they were getting married again, for the second time. And since last fall, they'd been happily ensconced in the cabin Jack had renovated for them on Butternut Lake, behaving, as Caroline had pointed out more than once, "like a couple of teenagers." Which was to say that even after almost four months of living together again, they could barely keep their hands off each other.

Jack looked troubled now though. It pained him, she knew, that they had lost so many years of what could have been their life together. It pained her, too, of course, but it pained Jack more, because he was the one—with his drinking, his gambling, and his womanizing—who was mainly responsible for the fact that those years had been lost to them. Two years ago, though, he'd gotten sober and straightened his life out, and now he was determined to make every single second count with Caroline, and with their daughter, Daisy, who was away at college.

"Jack, look," Caroline said. "I'm not bringing this up because I want you to feel guilty. I don't. But I want you to understand it from my perspective. The last time we got married, I was twenty-one. I was *a baby*, practically. And I had the skin to prove it. Then, when you left, I was twenty-four, still young, obviously, still no wrinkles on the horizon. You were gone, though, for almost two decades, and during that time, I went from being young to being middle-aged. And I can't help but think, what if you missed the best years of me? Not me as a person, I hope. But me as a woman. A woman who was attractive to you."

Jack said nothing, only studied her for a long moment before turning her around, slowly, until she was facing the mirror above her dresser, and he was standing behind her, his arms around her waist.

"I could tell you, Caroline, that you are as beautiful to me now as you were the day I met you, and it would be the truth. But I don't know if you're in the mood to believe me, so I'm going to show you something instead. I want you to look at yourself now," he said, gesturing at the mirror, "*really* look at yourself and—"

"*Jack, don't*," she said, feeling embarrassed, and twisting a little in his arms. Because despite the fact that she'd been looking in the mirror just a few minutes earlier, it wasn't something she spent a lot of time doing, and, when she did do it, it was almost always to examine something she was critical of. But now Jack held her, gently but firmly, and when she turned her face away from the mirror, he put his fingers, lightly, on her chin and turned it back.

"Look at yourself," he said, again, and she looked, reluctantly, into the mirror. "And don't just look at what you think is wrong with you," he said, "look at what I'm seeing right now. What I see every time I look at you." He ran his fingers through her strawberry-blond hair, which was shining in the lamplight, and which she'd always thought was her best feature. The feature she'd been happiest to pass on to Daisy, though Daisy had also gotten her blue eyes and her fair skin. And tonight, she had to admit, her eyes seemed especially blue and her fair skin seemed to be suffused with a soft glow.

In fact, looking in the mirror now, she saw what she thought Jack wanted her to see. She *did* look young. There was no sign of the gray hair that had recently started to appear—she'd found another one just that morning—or of the fine lines that had etched themselves around her eyes and her mouth. And maybe it was the forgiving light in the room, or the fact that Jack was looking at her reflection in the mirror with love, yes, but with desire, too, or maybe it was her own happiness at being with him, in a cabin he'd rebuilt for the two of them to live in together, but, whatever it was, she saw in herself now a certain kind of beauty. And if Jack was the only man who saw it, she realized, as well as the only man who could make her see it in herself, then that was just fine with her.

She turned to him now, sliding her hands up to his shoulders and kissing him, full on the mouth, and he pulled her against him and kissed her back, eventually sliding one of the slender straps of her nightgown off her shoulder, and caressing the bare skin there in a way that made Caroline think it was only a matter of seconds before he had that nightgown off altogether. But he surprised her, pulling away from her and looking down at the neckline of that nightgown and tracing one finger along it.

"You know, before we got back together," he said, "I used to dream—literally dream—about you wearing one of these nightgowns."

"You did?" Caroline said, surprised. She had several white cotton nightgowns like this one, and none of them, she thought, were particularly sexy. She'd bought them all, in fact, at the Variety Store in Butternut, all for $29.99 apiece. "Jack, why would you dream about me in some old nightgown?" she asked now, with amusement.

"Because you used to wear one when we were married the first time, and I always thought, on you anyway, that it was so beautiful. Any chance I could persuade you to wear one of them for our wedding ceremony?" he asked.

She shook her head. "Jack, I'm not getting married in front of fifty people in a nightgown," she said. "And anyway," she added, "I thought you liked the blue dress."

"I *love* the blue dress. I just love your nightgowns more," he said, his words soft against the hollow at the base of her neck. Caroline thought then about the dress she'd bought for the wedding, the dress that was hanging in her closet right now. It was a sleeveless, knee-length, pale blue silk dress with a white silk sash around the waist and a line of little pearl buttons up the back. She'd also had silk high-heeled shoes dyed to match it. It was, bar none, the prettiest outfit she'd ever owned.

"Well, *after* our wedding, I'll wear this nightgown,

maybe," she said. "In our room at the White Pines." The White Pines, where Caroline and Jack would be spending their wedding night, would also be the site of their ceremony and reception on Saturday, in three days, the day before Christmas Eve. The White Pines was a rustic but elegant resort, built in the 1930s out of wood and stone in a North Woods alpine style, and nestled on thirty acres of waterfront property on one of Butternut Lake's prettiest bays. Its ten cottages and its waterfront area—complete with fishing docks and boat rentals—were closed in the winter, but the main lodge, with its twenty-five rooms and its great room and dining room, both of which had a warm, clubby feeling and both of which overlooked the lake, was very much open. Caroline was in almost daily contact with Lori Pell, the director of the inn, about last-minute wedding details, and now, she remembered something.

"Oh, one second, honey," she said, reaching for a pencil and a little pad of paper that were on the dresser. She tried to keep these handy at all times so that she could scribble questions or ideas or reminders to herself about the wedding whenever they occurred to her. "We have to decide if we want a punch, a *nonalcoholic* punch, served at the reception," she said. "It would be in addition to the sparkling water, the fruit juice, and the soda. Lisa said the color would be a Christmas red, and that it would look pretty in the inn's antique punch bowl."

"That sounds nice," Jack said, watching as Caroline jotted down a note about it on the pad and then flipped it shut again.

"Now what were we talking about?" she asked, coming back into his arms.

"We weren't *talking* about anything," he said, kissing her again.

But then he remembered something, too. "What time does Daisy's bus get in tomorrow?" he asked.

"Twelve thirty," she said promptly, and she felt the little glow of pleasure she always felt at the prospect of Daisy coming home. She would be staying with them for almost three weeks on her winter break from the University of Minnesota in Minneapolis.

"Perfect," Jack said. "I'll pick her up."

"I wish I could come, too. But I can't leave Jessica to waitress alone during the lunch rush."

"No, you can't," Jack agreed. "And you don't need to. I'll bring Daisy straight over to Pearl's," he said, referring to the coffee shop that Caroline's family had opened in Butternut more than fifty years ago and that he was now a partner in as well.

"By the way," he asked, fiddling with her nightgown strap. "How is 'operation surprise Daisy' going?"

She smiled at the name he'd given this project. "It's not definite yet. We might not know right up until Christmas Eve morning. But if it all works out, it will be Daisy's best Christmas present ever," she said.

"It'd be a big surprise, all right," Jack agreed. But another wedding detail had popped into Caroline's head, and she reached for the pencil again and scribbled furiously onto the pad while Jack waited, a model of forbearance.

"I saw Joey at the IGA today," she explained to him,

dropping the pencil onto the dresser and coming back into his arms. "He asked if he could bring a plus one to the wedding, and I need to tell Lisa."

"I didn't know Joey had a girlfriend."

"He doesn't," she said, resting her cheek against the soft flannel of his shirt. "He has a boyfriend."

"Joey has a *boyfriend*?"

"Uh-huh," she said, running her hands up the front of his shirt. "You didn't know that?"

"No," he said. "I thought he was . . . you know, a guy's guy."

"He *is* a guy's guy."

"But, I mean . . ."

She smiled a little at his befuddlement. "What's the matter, Jack?" she teased. "Aren't you ready for the twenty-first century to reach Butternut?"

He kissed her, gently, on the lips. "I'm ready for anything," he said. "As long as I've got you in my life."

There was no more talking then, just kissing, and Jack sliding her nightgown's straps off her shoulders and letting the gown fall to the floor. No matter how much he liked it, apparently, he didn't want her wearing it anymore. And before she knew it, he'd maneuvered her over to the bed, too.

Jack had always been a fast worker that way, she thought, as she gave herself over to the sweet oblivion of the moment. Some things, it turned out, hadn't changed in the last eighteen years.

Chapter Two

Jack spent the next morning laying new floors in a cabin he was renovating. He'd bought the cabin in early fall, and though it had been in near-derelict condition, he'd planned to do the same thing to it he'd done to his and Caroline's cabin; namely, rebuild it from the outside in. The work was going well, and if he could sell it in the spring, at a healthy profit, he planned on making a business out of renovating cabins on the lake.

But despite his busy morning, he still left himself plenty of time to drive to the bus stop to pick up Daisy. So much time, in fact, that he was there half an hour early. He didn't mind, though. Being a real father to his daughter was still new to him, and he was determined to do it "right," even though the meaning of that word sometimes eluded him. Being an alcoholic had taught him how to be a drinking buddy, a casual lover, and a fair-weather friend, but it had taught him almost nothing about how to be a good husband and a good father. Now, after being two years sober, he was just learning this, and there were times when he felt a sudden sense of insecurity and self-doubt. Had he said the right thing? Had he done the right thing? Had he been the man they needed him to be? The man *he* needed to be for *them*?

But all these thoughts fell away the moment he saw Daisy get off the bus. "Hey," he said, scooping her up in his arms and swinging her around. "You're home."

"I'm home, Dad," Daisy agreed. "And I missed you so much." She sounded like herself, the self that Jack thought was just about perfect, but when he set her down and took a closer look at her, she didn't look like herself. Not entirely. She looked thinner, and her blue eyes were shadowed with fatigue, her pale skin almost translucent.

"Daisy, what's wrong?" he asked.

"Nothing's wrong," she assured him, as the bus driver opened the baggage compartment and Jack took her suitcase out. They thanked the driver then, and Jack carried her suitcase over to his pickup and sat it down in the flatbed.

"Dad, I'm fine," Daisy said, as they both climbed into the truck. "Really," she insisted, seeing the worried expression on his face. "It's just . . ."

"It's just what?" he asked, turning on the ignition so the heat would be on in the truck, but making no move to drive away.

"I don't know, it's just . . . everything," she said, with a helpless shrug.

Jack said nothing, but he knew what Daisy meant by "everything." She meant Will Hughes. Will was Daisy's boyfriend. Her first serious boyfriend. They'd gone to high school together, though they'd been in different worlds there. Daisy, the straight A student and gifted athlete, and Will, the perennial bad boy, irresistible to girls, but, alas, not to the administrators and teachers at their school. Last summer, though, to everyone's surprise, Daisy's and Will's worlds had intersected—or, in Caroline's mind, collided—and the two of them had been inseparable. When Will had told Daisy at the end of the summer that he was joining the army, she'd been almost inconsolable. And Will, it turned out, hadn't been much better, though there hadn't been any tears on his part, just a stoic misery that Jack had recognized immediately. It was that same misery that had kept him company on those late nights, and those early mornings, after he'd given up drinking, but before he knew if he would ever get his wife and daughter back again.

"Hey," Jack said gently, watching the bus drive away. "I know what it's like to miss someone."

Daisy nodded, and, as she snuggled deeper into her down jacket, she suddenly looked much younger than her twenty-one years. "Did it ever get better?" she asked.

Jack sighed, considered lying, then changed his mind. "No, not until I was with you and your mother again," he said. And, for a moment, he almost told her about the surprise they were planning for her. But it wasn't definite yet, and to get her hopes up now only to dash them later seemed especially cruel. So he pulled on his seat belt and shifted the truck into drive, then glanced over at Daisy, and said, "We better get going. Your mom's expecting us for lunch at Pearl's, and I promised Jessica you'd have a hot chocolate with her afterward."

"That sounds good," Daisy said, as Jack pulled out onto the highway. And then, "How's Mom?"

"Mom's good," he said. "Excited to see you, of course."

"And busy with the wedding plans?" Daisy asked, looking out the window at the snowy landscape sliding by. And there was something about the way she said this, and looked away from him as she said it, that gave Jack pause.

"She's very excited about the wedding," he said carefully. "But I'm getting the impression you're not."

"Oh, no, I am excited," Daisy said emphatically, turning to him. "I'm thrilled you two are getting remarried, Dad. I don't have *any* reservations about that. But this wedding Mom's planned, I have to say, honestly, it doesn't sound like her at all. And it *definitely* doesn't sound like you. I mean, the fancy clothes, and the tiered cake and the sit-down dinner—is that really your kind of thing? I thought if you got married again you two would do something like, you know . . ."

"Fly to Las Vegas?"

"No, not that. But something smaller. Something . . . I don't know, intimate. And, and not casual, maybe. But not fancy, either."

"I'm not sure you can call this wedding 'fancy.'"

"Well, by Butternut standards it is."

"Maybe," Jack allowed. "But that's not saying much. Besides, it's not like we're breaking the bank here. You'd be amazed how much less a reception costs when you're not serving alcohol."

"I don't mean the money, though, Dad. I mean . . . what do you want?"

"I want to be married to your mother."

"No, what kind of *wedding* do you want?"

"Oh, that's easy," he said. "I want whatever kind of wedding your mom wants."

"So this is about Mom being happy?"

"Well, yes, to a point. But it's about more than that, too. It's about rewriting history. Which is something you don't get to do very often in life."

"What do you mean?" she asked, turning toward him.

He hesitated. "When your mom and I got married the first time, it wasn't exactly her dream wedding. Her parents hated me, for one thing, so there was no happy family to celebrate with us. And we were broke, for another. Neither of us had any savings yet, and her parents didn't want to spend any of their money because . . . well, as I said, they hated me. So we put something together. Your mom bought a dress on sale, and her family's minister married us in a small service at Lutheran Redeemer. At the last minute, your great-grandmother relented, a little, and made some iced tea and finger sandwiches for guests to have in the church basement after the ceremony." (Jack didn't mention here that in a twist of fate this was the same church basement where he now attended his AA meetings.)

"Anyway," he continued, "is it so surprising that your mom wanted something different this time around? Something that felt more . . . special, I guess. More permanent."

His mind caught on that word now. *Permanent.* The marriage that had followed that wedding, of course, had been anything but. And if Caroline wanted something else this time around, how could he blame her? Because while he might not feel that strongly about the details of the wedding, he felt very strongly about the marriage that came after it. "Permanent" was what he had in mind now. And while the whole "till death do us part" thing had always seemed unnecessarily morbid to him, it didn't seem that way anymore.

"Aren't you forgetting something, Dad?"

"What?" he asked, slowing down on the highway to let another car pass them. He always drove conservatively when Daisy was in the pickup with him.

"Aren't you leaving something out of the whole first wedding story? You know, the part about Mom already being pregnant with me?"

The truck swerved so slightly it was barely noticeable. "I . . . didn't think you knew about that."

"Well, I do," she said, looking amused.

"Your mom doesn't think you know, either."

"Don't worry," Daisy said. "I won't tell her."

"When did you, umm . . ."

"As soon as I was old enough to count," Daisy said, archly. "No, not really. When I was about twelve, I think, I was helping Mom organize some papers and I came across your marriage certificate. I realized it was dated six months before I was born. But she'd never told me, so I figured she didn't want me to know."

"It's not like that," Jack said, turning off the highway

and onto a county road. "I think she was afraid if you knew you weren't planned, you might think, wrongly, that we weren't as thrilled about your arrival as we might have been otherwise. But we were, trust me. That wedding might not have been perfect, but you, Daisy, you were perfect. Even though you were still just a tiny bump under your mom's wedding dress, you were already the best thing that either of us would ever do."

"Dad, stop," Daisy said, brushing at the corner of one of her eyes. "You're going to make me cry."

Jack smiled at her. "No crying, all right?" he said as he drove past the BUTTERNUT, POPULATION 1,200 sign. "Your mom will not be happy with me if I bring you into Pearl's and you're already in tears."

"No crying," she agreed, looking out the window at the sight of a town so familiar to her that Jack thought she could probably reconstruct every detail of it with her eyes closed. But at this time of year, of course, Butternut was all dressed up in its Christmas finery, and as they turned down Main Street, Daisy let out a little cry of pleasure.

"I forgot how pretty Butternut is at Christmastime," she said, and even Jack, who'd once chafed at a town he'd considered gossipy and small-minded, had to admit that it did Christmas right. The sidewalks on Main Street were lined, at twenty-foot intervals, with Christmas trees hung with colored lights, and an enormous lighted wreath was strung on wires over the street's main intersection. Then there were all the storefronts—Butternut Drugs, Johnson's hardware, and the Pine Cone Gallery among them—which were also strung with lights and hung with wreaths.

But it was Pearl's, Jack thought, easing the pickup truck into a parking space right in front, that was the crown jewel of Butternut. Part coffee shop, part town hall, and part gossip clearinghouse, it was the one indispensable business in this town. And it was decorated like it knew it. The brightly polished windows were adorned with strands of tiny white twinkling lights, and its front door sported a lush green wreath with a big red bow on it. Through the windows, Jack could see the miniature red and white poinsettias on each table, and, from the ceiling, the big shiny gold stars that hung down, rotating gently in the draft from the opening and closing front door.

"Oh, look, Mom put out that sleigh," Daisy said, pointing at the entryway table where a miniature Santa's sleigh and eight miniature reindeer were set up. "I used to spend hours playing with that when I was little. And it shows, too. Last Christmas I noticed it was definitely a little worse for wear."

"I'm sure that's just part of its charm now," Jack said, as he cut the ignition and put the truck in park. "But Pearl's looks nice, doesn't it? We spent the Friday night after Thanksgiving decorating it. It helped, of course, that Frankie is so tall he didn't have to stand on a ladder to hang those stars." Frankie was the fry cook, manager, and now, part owner of Pearl's. Jack unfastened his seat belt and reached for the door handle. "You ready?" he asked when Daisy made no move to join him.

"Do we have to go in yet?" she asked. "Could we stay here a little longer?"

"Sure," he said, glancing at his watch. "Your mom's not

expecting us for another five minutes. Why? What's up?" he asked, as he turned the ignition and the heat back on.

Daisy sighed. "Nothing's up; I just want to mentally prepare myself."

"For Pearl's?" Jack said, bemused. "I wasn't aware that eating there required any mental preparation. I mean, the menu's still pretty straightforward."

Daisy laughed. "No, I mean, everyone in there will know me, and know everything about me, including at least five embarrassing stories from my childhood. And they'll know what position I played on the volleyball team in high school, and what my grade point average was, and who I dated."

"The burdens of celebrityhood?" Jack teased.

Daisy smiled. "The burdens of living in a small town. Because I'm not unique. Believe me, I'll know as much about everyone else in Pearl's as they'll know about me. I just want to get ready for it, that's all. All that familiarity. All that . . . concern."

"Should we be concerned?"

"No," Daisy said, shaking her head. "I'm fine."

"You know, honey, every time you say 'I'm fine,' I feel a little less convinced that you're fine."

She laughed again, and Jack savored the sound of it. Making his daughter laugh had become one of his great pleasures in life.

"No, I mean it, Dad," Daisy said now. "I'm just tired."

"From taking exams?" he asked.

She nodded.

"But they went well, right?"

"They did. Even abnormal psychology, which I was dreading. The professor is really intense. *Abnormally* intense," she added, with a smile.

"Is that the class you study serial killers in?"

"No, Dad, sorry. It's not like *Criminal Minds*."

"I do like that show, though."

"Well, take heart then. Because I'm taking criminal psychology next semester."

"Now *that* sounds interesting," he said. "And how is Will, by the way?" he asked. "I mean, other than the fact that he can't be in the same state as you." Will was stationed at Fort Eustis, in Virginia, where he'd been sent after basic training to attend Aviation Logistics school.

"Well, let's see," Daisy said, "he hates the five thirty A.M. wake-up call, he hates the food, which he says Mom would not let within a mile of Pearl's, and he hates the fact that the guy who sleeps above him snores so loudly it makes the whole bunk bed vibrate. But you know what? He *loves* the AH-64A Apache helicopter."

"Is that what he's being trained to work on?"

She nodded. "Right now, he's studying engine disassembly and repair. And whenever he talks about it, he sounds like a little kid who just got a new toy truck or something. If the Apache helicopter were a woman, I'd be in trouble. I'm almost jealous as it is."

"They're pretty cool," Jack agreed.

"With a price tag of fifty-two million dollars, they should be cool."

Jack whistled softly. "That's a lot of tuna melts," he said, glancing over at Pearl's, where the afternoon rush seemed to be winding down. "Listen, we better get going, okay? Your mom's reserved your favorite back booth for your homecoming lunch."

"Okay," Daisy said. "I'm ready to face the music. And, Dad?"

"Yes."

"About the wedding. You're right. Mom should have the wedding she wants to have. She's earned it."

"That was my thinking exactly," Jack said, reaching for the door handle.

Chapter Three

"Daisy, have you lost weight?" Jessica asked, frowning, as they sat at the counter at Pearl's later that afternoon, sipping hot chocolates. Nat King Cole's "The Christmas Song" was playing on the radio behind the counter, and the gold stars that hung from the ceiling twirled slowly above their heads.

Daisy sighed. She'd already deflected this question about her weight from her mother during lunch, but she hadn't expected it from Jessica. Was *everyone* going to worry about her? she wondered a little irritably. But then she noticed the expression of concern on Jessica's pretty heart-shaped face, and she softened. Jessica and her parents were only worried about her because they cared about her, she reminded herself. And she *had* lost weight, it was true. But she hadn't tried to. It had just . . . happened.

"It's missing Will, isn't it?" Jessica asked now, tucking

a glossy brown curl behind one ear. "That's why you can't eat, isn't it?"

"I can eat. I *do* eat. But honestly, it just seems like so much work. *Everything* seems like so much work. Except Will."

"How do you two stay in touch?" Jessica asked.

"It's hard," Daisy admitted. "He wakes up at five A.M., starts his physical training by five thirty, has breakfast at seven, and then has classes all day until dinnertime. He gets one hour of personal time from eight thirty to nine thirty P.M., so that's usually when we talk, but he has two roommates, so we don't have a lot of privacy. There's also no Wi-Fi in his barracks, only a computer in their common room that they can sign up to Skype on. So we do that whenever we get the chance. But mostly, we write letters."

Daisy stirred her hot chocolate, thinking of the last letter she'd gotten from Will. It had literally made her blush, though blush in a good way. "You know," she confided to Jessica, "Will had never written a letter before he started writing to me. I mean, it was always just him and his dad in their family and his dad isn't the kind of guy you'd want to stay in touch with, anyway. But it turns out Will's pretty good at writing them." So good, in fact, that Daisy had letters from him she'd reread so many times that their pages were coming apart at the creases. "It's not enough, though," she said now. "None of it is. No matter how hard we try, it's just not the same as being able to reach out and touch each other."

Jessica nodded, her brown eyes sympathetic. "That part must be so hard, Daisy. I mean, Frankie and I touch each other all the time and it's *still* not enough." Daisy stared into her cup of hot chocolate and said nothing. She didn't want to encourage this line of conversation. She loved Jessica—her sweet but scatterbrained best friend from childhood—and she loved Frankie—equally sweet, but practically gargantuan in size—but she preferred not to think of them together. At least, not in *that* way. Some things, it turned out, were best left unimagined.

"Daisy," Jessica said, looking around and lowering her voice, though the few customers lingering over their late lunches weren't sitting anywhere near them. "Do you and Will ever, you know, sext?"

Daisy shook her head. "No. Will can't have a cell phone during training. But, God knows, there've been times when I've thought if he did have one, I'd be willing to try it," she admitted. Times when being separated from Will had begun to feel like an almost physical pain to her. "But honestly, Jessica, even if I could sext, I don't think I'd do it. I'm not much of an exhibitionist, and Will doesn't seem like one either. And then there's . . . there's that picture of my great grandma Pearl. You know, the one hanging in my mom's office? I think of it, and I think, 'that woman would not have approved of me taking pictures of myself with my clothes off.'"

Jessica nodded. "I've seen that picture, Daisy. And your great grandma Pearl doesn't look like she would have approved of *anything*. At least not anything fun. But you're going to see Will soon, aren't you, in just a few months?"

"In two months."

"Daisy, you say two *months* like it's two *years*."

Daisy smiled, a little tiredly, and reached for the can of whipped cream on the counter between them and gave what was left of her hot chocolate another generous squirt of it. "Do you want some pie, too?" Jessica asked. "I think there's still a piece of apple left."

"No, thanks," Daisy said, "I had the special for lunch," the special being her favorite sandwich at Pearl's, the French dip. "I don't know why I'm even eating this," she said, spooning the whipped cream off her hot chocolate and into her mouth.

"No, it's good," Jessica said. "*Keep* eating. We'll fatten you up in no time."

"Hmm, Pearl's is good at doing that," Daisy observed. They sat in silence for a few minutes, and when Daisy had finished off her whipped cream, Jessica slid off her stool and went around to the other side of the counter and got a soup bowl out and filled that with whipped cream, too. Then she pushed it, determinedly, over to Daisy. "Keep going," she said, in a stern voice, or at least in as stern a voice as someone who was as sweet as Jessica could muster—and Daisy laughed and dug her spoon into that, too.

"How've *you* been, Jessica?" she asked her friend, between bites. "I know you and Frankie are still going strong, but what about everything else?"

"You mean, like work?"

Daisy nodded, though this was another topic she hoped not to dwell on. She had gotten Jessica a waitressing job at Pearl's last summer, after Jessica had flunked out of cosmetology school. But things had never gone smoothly for her here, and they both knew that if she weren't Daisy's best friend, Caroline would have fired her long ago.

"Work's going better," Jessica said. "Really, it is. Frankie helps me out whenever he can, and your mom, your mom has been in such a good mood since she and your dad got back together. Even when I do make a mistake, she almost never loses her temper at me. These last few weeks, though, she's been a little stressed out about the wedding. But I can't blame her. I mean, who wouldn't be, right?" And then Jessica blushed, and, leaning closer to Daisy, she whispered, "Can you keep a secret?"

"Of course."

"Well . . ." Jessica reached down the front of her blouse and fished out a gold chain, at the end of which was a ring. She held it out to Daisy, and Daisy saw, on closer inspection, that it was an engagement ring, though the diamond set in it was modest in size. No, not modest. Small. There was really no other word for it. It was just . . . *small*. "I know the diamond's not very big," Jessica said, quickly, almost peremptorily. "It's only a third of a carat. But it's what Frankie can afford right now. He bought a share in your mom's business, and he's helping support his sister, but he says there'll be another ring one day. This is just to hold me until then."

And Daisy, feeling a rush of guilt for dwelling, first and foremost, on the diamond's size, instead of on what it represented for Jessica and Frankie, pulled her friend into a hug. "It's beautiful, Jessica," she said, honestly. "I'm so happy for you two. Really, I couldn't be any happier."

Her eyes filled with tears then, and all at once she felt it, the happiness for Jessica and Frankie, yes, but also the fatigue, the stress, and the aching loneliness of the last several months. She gave Jessica a final squeeze and let go of her right as Frankie, who'd been meeting with her mother in Pearl's back office, came through the coffee shop's back door and looked at the two of them quizzically. By now, Jessica was crying, too.

"I told her," Jessica explained, pulling some napkins out of the napkin dispenser on the counter and wiping her eyes. "And she's sworn to secrecy." Daisy nodded and then she got up and went around to the other side of the counter to hug a pleased but slightly abashed Frankie. Hugging Frankie was never easy—Daisy could barely get her arms around him—but she did the best she could and he hugged her back and explained quietly, "We decided to keep it on the down low. At least until after your parents' wedding. After that, we'll make an announcement or something."

Jessica settled the chain with the engagement ring on it back inside of her blouse, and Frankie joined them at the counter where the three of them talked as the last few customers paid their bills and drifted out of Pearl's. But when Frankie left to check the walk-in fridge's inventory for the next day, Jessica jumped up and said excitedly, "I have to show you something else. It's another secret, but this one I'm keeping from Frankie, too." She disappeared into the stockroom and returned with a big shopping bag. "I'm teaching myself how to knit," she explained. "So I can make Frankie a Christmas present. What do you think?" She held up an enormous bundle of red wool and then shook it out and let it unfurl itself all the way to the floor. It was of an indeterminate shape, and it had more than a few dropped stitches in it, but Daisy, understanding what it was, tried to focus on the positive. "Jessica, it's amazing. Frankie will love having a blanket like that to keep him warm on cold winter nights."

"Oh no, it's not a blanket," Jessica said, surprised. "It's a sweater."

Chapter Four

THAT NIGHT, AS Jack and Caroline and Daisy were sitting down to dinner at their cabin, Caroline's friend Allie
was about to undertake an almost herculean task at hers;
namely, persuading her nine-year-old son, Wyatt, to go
to sleep. Fortunately, she had enough experience doing
this to know that the best line of attack to take was an
indirect one. Which was why she leaned, casually, on his
open bedroom door now and asked, "Mind if I come in?"

"Nope," he said, though he didn't look up from the
floor where he was sitting, in his pajamas, hard at work
on one of his Lego creations.

"What're you building?" she asked, coming over and
sitting down, a little awkwardly, on the rug beside him.
It was only now, eight and a half months into her pregnancy, that she was beginning to feel—as her friend Jax
would say—"seriously pregnant."

"It's a twin-blade helicopter," Wyatt said, glancing over at her.

"It looks pretty complicated," she said, sifting her fingers through the Lego pieces that were scattered around them on the rug.

"It is."

"You know, Daisy's boyfriend, Will, is learning how to repair real helicopters in the army," Allie offered.

She had his full attention now. "I know," he said. "Caroline told me. Do you think . . ." He paused to snap a piece of a propeller in place. "Do you think I can ask him about it the next time I see him?"

"Oh, absolutely," Allie said, resisting the urge to reach over and tousle his curly brown hair. Since entering the fourth grade Wyatt had discouraged this old habit of Allie's, and she missed doing it. Just like she missed holding his hand in public and tucking him into bed at night. But Wyatt was firm about his new maturity, and Allie was trying, very hard, to respect it. "I think Will would be happy to answer all your questions about helicopters," she said. "I'm not sure when he'll be back in Butternut, though."

Wyatt nodded, still working, and Allie watched him for a few more minutes, wondering when the precise moment was that Wyatt had transferred his passion from train sets to Legos.

"All right," she said, looking at her watch. "I'm going to leave you to finish this up. Jax and Caroline are coming over later, and I want to make hot mulled cider for them.

But Wyatt? You need to be in bed no later than nine o'clock. Walker will come in and remind you, okay?"

He nodded, and then put down his Lego piece and stood up. "I think I'll just get into bed now," he said. "I'm pretty exhausted, actually."

"Oh," Allie said, trying to repress a smile and wondering what it was about his day, exactly, that had been so exhausting. Still, she was so relieved that he was going to bed without a fight that she was practically giddy. "Do you need anything?" she asked, standing up. "A glass of milk, maybe?"

"Nope. Just my sweatshirt," he said, walking over to his dresser, opening the bottom drawer, and pulling out a faded maroon-and-gold University of Minnesota sweatshirt, size men's large. She watched as he tugged it over his head. It was so big on him that the hand holes hung empty at his sides, and the bottom swung down around his knees. But Wyatt loved it just the same. It had belonged to his father, Gregg, Allie's late husband, who had been killed in Afghanistan five years ago, and Wyatt liked to wear it to bed in cold weather, and, sometimes, it turned out, in warm weather, too. Walker, Allie's second husband and now Wyatt's adoptive father, had never felt threatened by this, by this or by any of the ways in which she and Wyatt kept Gregg's memory alive. Not all the adjustments their new little family had had to make over the past three and a half years had been easy, but this one had been. Now, of course, there would be another adjustment, she thought, running a hand over her belly.

She watched as Wyatt scrambled into bed, then said, "You can read for a little while if you want to."

He shook his head. "I finished *Harry Potter and the Goblet of Fire*," he said, indicating the book on his bedside table.

"Are you going to read the next one?"

"Not yet. I just want to think about this one for a little while longer. You know, remember it?"

"I know," Allie said. "And it's a good policy." *Especially since the fifth book*, Harry Potter and the Order of the Phoenix, *is wrapped and sitting under our Christmas tree right now.* "Good night, honey," she said, starting to leave the room. But when she got to the door, Wyatt called her back.

"Mom?"

"Uh-huh?"

"I don't really need you to tuck me in anymore, but if you *really* want to, this one time, you could."

"I *really* want to," Allie said, smiling, and she came and sat down on the edge of his bed and started the old routine of tucking him in—plumping up the pillows, straightening out the sheets, and pulling the blanket up.

"Mom?"

"Yes?"

"What was Christmas like for us when Dad was still alive?"

"It was . . . it was good," she said. "Really good." *Do you remember the last one?* she almost said, but she caught herself and instead changed it to "Do you remember the one when you were three?"

"A little," he said. "Is that the year I got the swing set?"

"That was the year. Your dad had so much fun picking

it out." And then she remembered another present. "Do you know what he gave you the Christmas you were one year old?"

He shook his head.

"A basketball."

"A basketball? When I was one? What was I supposed to do with it?"

"You know what? That was the same question I asked your dad. But when you unwrapped it, with a little help from him, you seemed to like it. Mainly, though, you tried to eat the wrapping paper. It was Dad who ended up practicing free throws with it on Christmas morning."

"Do you think he knew then I'd be a good basketball player?" he asked. He played now on a youth basketball team that Walker coached.

"I know he did," Allie said seriously.

Wyatt nodded, seemingly satisfied, and when she reached over to stroke his hair, he let her. She wondered, after a few minutes, if he'd fall asleep like this, as he'd done so often when he was younger. But suddenly he said, "You know what Jade told me?" Jade was Allie's friend Jax's ten-year-old daughter.

"What?"

"She told me that when the baby's born, it'll ruin everything."

"Jade said that?" Allie asked in surprise. "But, Wyatt, she loves Jenna." Jenna was Jade's three-year-old sister. "I don't honestly think she believes that Jenna being born ruined everything."

"Well, maybe not forever," Wyatt conceded. "But

for a while, anyway. I mean, she said Jenna cried all the time, which kept everyone awake at night. And she said her mom was always tired, and her dad couldn't do that much fun stuff with her and her sisters anymore 'cause he had to help their mom, and everything was different than it was before. Like, not as good as it was before."

"Well, Jade's right about one thing, Wyatt. Things *are* going to change. I mean, the baby will cry, though hopefully not so loudly that it'll wake you up at night, especially when you consider what a sound sleeper you are. And I probably will be tired, at least at first, and Walker probably will be less fun. But, Wyatt, none of those things will last forever. The baby will settle down, and I'll get more sleep, and Walker will have more time to do things with you, and then the good part will start."

"The good part?"

She nodded. "That's right. Because your brother or your sister is going to need you. They're going to count on you one day. And they're going to look up to you, too. You might think they're a pain in the neck sometimes, but they are going to think you're the coolest person in the world."

"They are?" he said, perking up.

"Absolutely. Just ask Walker. He *worshipped* his older brother, Reid, when he was a kid. And who wouldn't have? Reid taught him how to do things, and helped him with his homework, and told him ghost stories, and all that fun stuff. Walker loves me and you very much, and he'll love the baby very much, too, but he'll always love Reid in a different way. A special way. Because Reid's his older brother."

Wyatt seemed pleased, but also, Allie thought, a little daunted. "Is there a book about how to be an older brother?" he asked.

"There are many of them. And I've been meaning to get you some, too. Why don't we stop by the library the next time we're in town and you can choose some, okay? But the main way you're going to learn how to be an older brother is just by being one. And you're going to be a *really* good one."

"I think you're right," Wyatt said, regaining his confidence.

Allie bent down and kissed him on the forehead. "I'm going to say good night now. Oh, and don't forget, it's supposed to snow overnight. So I definitely see some fort building in your future. I'll send Walker in to say his good night now, okay?"

She started to get up.

"Mom," he said, quickly, "can I ask Walker if he'll still take me fishing after the baby's born?"

"You can ask him," Allie said, smiling, and reached down to ruffle his curls again. "But I think you already know the answer. You're not just a son to him, Wyatt. You're also the best fishing buddy he's ever had."

"CAN I HAVE some of that?" Walker asked, watching as Allie stirred a pot of hot mulled cider on the stove later that night.

"You can. But you'll have to take it upstairs with you. Caroline and Jax are going to be here soon, and you know the rules." The "rules" Allie was referring to were the rules for the monthly "girls' night in" that Allie and Caroline and Jax had been having since the summer she and Wyatt had moved to Butternut three and a half years ago. There were no husbands or children allowed, and there was no set agenda, either, other than to have a good time.

"I know the rules," Walker agreed, as Allie ladled cider into a mug and handed it to him. "Just, um . . . just don't overdo it tonight, okay?"

"Overdo it?" Allie repeated, slipping potholders on and lifting a pan of gingerbread cake out of the oven.

"You know what I mean," Walker said, a little sheepishly.

"So no Jell-O shots?" Allie clarified. "No dancing on the furniture? What about cigars and an all-night game of Texas Hold'em?"

"All right, I get it," Walker said. "I worry too much. I'm leaving now." Then, eyeing the gingerbread cake, he asked, "Any chance I can take a piece of that with me?"

"Now you're pressing your luck," she said, but when he turned to leave, she made him come back and hold her. "You know, in a way, I'll miss being pregnant," she said. "But I won't miss this. I won't miss not being able to get any closer to you than this." She nodded at her belly, wedged firmly between them. But at that moment, she heard a car pull up outside.

"Go," she said.

"I will. I love you," he said, kissing her quickly, picking his mug up off the counter, and heading out of the kitchen.

"I love you, too," she called after him, and then she was opening the front door to Caroline and Jax and an icy blast of wind. "Your timing's perfect," she said, hugging them as they came into the bright, warm kitchen, which was now filled with the deliciously spicy smells of cloves and ginger. "Let me take your things," she offered, but Caroline and Jax were already shrugging off their coats and hats and gloves, and piling them, and their purses, on one of the kitchen chairs.

"I can't stay long," Caroline apologized. "It's Daisy's first night back. But the three of us have had dinner, and I've left her and Jack watching some show—some godawful police procedural about tracking serial killers—so I can spend at least an hour with you ladies."

"I've got to get back, too," Jax said, coming over to watch as Allie filled three more mugs with cider. "I promised Jeremy I'd leave before the snow started. Well, that, and I have about a jillion presents to wrap."

"A jillion?" Allie said, slicing the gingerbread cake. "You know, Jax, if anyone else said that, I might think it was a slight exaggeration. But in your case, it's probably right on the money."

"Speaking of money," Jax said, as Allie lifted slices of gingerbread cake out of the pan and arranged them on a platter. "Having four daughters at Christmastime is costing us a *fortune*. Jeremy told the girls about how his dad grew up on a farm, one of ten children, and how every Christmas they each got exactly one present. Funnily enough, though, none of our girls were interested in doing that in our family."

"It's just as well," Caroline said, coming over to join them. "Because, let's face it, that one present would have to be one heck of a present."

Allie chuckled as she put the cider and gingerbread onto a tray.

"Actually," Jax said, "I don't mind all the presents. As long as we can avoid another Christmas like the one we had when Joy was in the third grade and some boy on her school bus told her Santa Claus wasn't real. Of course, she couldn't wait to get home and break the news to her younger sisters, who basically cried until Christmas, which at that point was still a week away. Now, though, with Jenna"—Jenna, at three, was Jax's youngest daughter—"me and Jeremy and the girls are all on the same page. And we've decided that Jenna is going to go to college believing in Santa Claus. Here, let me take that." She took the tray Allie had set, and though it wasn't very heavy, Allie let her carry it to the living room.

But Jax stopped at the room's threshold. "Martha Stewart, eat your heart out," she said delightedly, and Allie had to admit, the room was magical at this time of year. Walker had built this cabin before he'd met Allie and Wyatt, and the centerpiece of it had been the living room, with its cathedral ceilings, enormous fieldstone fireplace, and floor-to-ceiling windows overlooking Butternut Lake below. Now, with the Christmas season upon them, there was a twelve-foot blue spruce tree in one corner of the room, decorated with brightly colored lights and ornaments, and on all the tabletops, and on the banister to the staircase leading up to the second floor, there were lush and beribboned pine garlands. But it was the huge fireplace, which was crackling with fragrant pine and birch logs—and its wide mantelpiece, which was covered with an elaborate, miniature, snowy village—that really drew the eye to it.

"Honestly, Allie," Jax said, setting the tray on the coffee table and flinging herself down on one of the deep, cognac-colored leather couches that flanked the fireplace. "I don't know why you and Walker insist on referring to this place as a 'cabin' when we all know it's really much more of a 'castle.'" Allie looked over at her friend and marveled, not for the first time, at Jax's youthfulness. She was thirty-four, the same age as Allie, but with her petite build and physical quickness, she still reminded Allie of a teenager. Jax had, in fact, *been* a teenager when Allie, whose family had summered at Butternut Lake, had met her for the first time. A lot had changed in both of their lives since then, but Jax still wore her shiny black hair in the same ponytail and still had the same riotously freckled complexion she'd had at sixteen.

"I'm not sure this place is a 'castle,'" Allie said now, as she and Caroline settled onto the couch opposite Jax. "But it does feel big to me now. Too big. Especially when I try to clean it."

"You're going to have help, aren't you?" Caroline asked, serving herself a piece of gingerbread.

"Yes, Lonnie Haagan, Walker's housekeeper from his bachelor days, is already here part-time. In fact, she made this gingerbread cake batter right before she left this evening."

Caroline took a bite of it now and sighed with pleasure. "Tell her to have a whole pan of it waiting for you when you come home from the hospital. Which reminds me," she said, "how's everything going, now that you're in the homestretch?"

"I feel good," Allie said, lounging back on the couch. "A little heavy, a little slow, and a little tired, maybe, but you two know the drill, right?"

"Well, Jax knows it better than I do," Caroline remarked, and Jax, who was happily ensconced on the couch across from them, threw her an affectionate look.

"The only thing that's bothering me," Allie said, sipping her cider, "is that Walker's being so . . . *so protective* of me."

"That's bothering you?" Jax said.

"No, not the protectiveness. I don't mean that. I mean . . . what's behind it."

Jax frowned.

"He's afraid that something's going to go wrong," Allie said. "Something serious." And she glanced, reflexively, at the stairs, but there was no sign of Walker.

"Did he tell you this?" Caroline asked. She'd slipped off her shoes and tucked her legs up underneath her on the couch.

"No, not in so many words. But he doesn't need to. He has insomnia, first off, something he only gets when he's worried about something. Half the time I wake up at night and he's not even there. He's downstairs. On his computer. And the rest of the time, he tiptoes around me like I'm breakable. Like I'm a Fabergé egg that's about to be dropped."

They were all silent for a moment, until Caroline said, gently, "Well, you can't blame him, can you? All he has to draw on here is his past experience."

And Allie sighed, because Caroline was right, of course. Walker's ex-wife, Caitlin, had lost their baby when she was six months pregnant, and Walker, she knew, had always held himself partly to blame for this. He and Caitlin had gotten married because she was pregnant, and, afterward, when it became apparent to Walker how little they had in common, he'd retreated into his work. Caitlin had been desperately lonely, Walker had later learned, and desperately unhappy, and no amount of persuasion on anyone's part had ever been able to convince him that this hadn't contributed, in some way, to the fact that one chilly fall day, the baby's heart had simply stopped beating.

"No, I don't blame him," Allie said now, softly, and Jax, perhaps sensing that the mood in the room had become too somber, suddenly popped up on the couch and said, "I think a toast is in order."

"What are we toasting to?" Caroline asked, reaching for her spiced cider.

"We're toasting to *you*," Jax said, "our bride-to-be. Because this is your last girls' night in as a single woman."

"I'll drink to that," Allie said, grabbing her mug. "As long as you promise you're still going to come to these."

"Are you kidding?" Caroline said, clinking mugs with them. "I'll be at every single one."

"Hmm, we might want you to put that in writing," Jax said. "Because Allie and I did not see that much of you after you and Jack first got back together. In fact, I was starting to wonder if you two were ever going to get out of bed."

Caroline blushed. "We're getting much better about that, actually."

"Are you, really?"

"No," she said. "But we're working on it. Especially now that Daisy's home. I mean, let's face it"—she licked a gingerbread crumb off her finger—"nobody wants to think about their parents being in love. It's just too . . . unsettling."

"It's true," Jax agreed. "Whenever Jeremy and I kiss in front of our daughters, the younger ones shriek hysterically, and the older ones roll their eyes as if to say, 'Really? Aren't you two getting a little old for that?' As in 'completely ancient, way-beyond-sex too old?'"

Allie smiled and shifted around on the coach, trying to get more comfortable. "Seriously, though, how is Daisy?" she asked Caroline.

Caroline sighed. "Too thin, too pale, and too . . . too world-weary for someone her age."

"Still, that's got to be hard," Allie sympathized. "Any word yet on the surprise for Daisy . . ."

"Nothing definite," Caroline said, with a little shake of her head. It was quiet in the room for a moment.

"She must be excited about the wedding, though," Allie prompted.

"I think she is," Caroline said, smiling, but then something seemed to occur to her and she jumped up and rushed to the kitchen, and then rushed back, a notepad and pencil in her hands. "I try to keep this in my purse at all times," she explained, opening up the notebook and scribbling into it. "That way, if I remember anything I still need to do, I put it in here. Tomorrow, for instance, I have to give Lori Pell my decision about whether to have prime rib or beef Wellington at the reception."

"What kind of cake did you end up choosing?" Allie asked. The three of them and Jack had spent a memorable afternoon tasting wedding cakes at a bakery in Ely.

"A two-tiered buttercream cake with vanilla frosting and pink buttercream roses on it."

"Oh, it'll look so pretty. And what did you decide about the bouquet? Is it going to be the white gardenias or the white amaryllis and white roses?"

"The white amaryllis," Caroline said, flipping her notebook closed and suddenly looking as if she was about sixteen. "I'm having the best time doing all this," she added, curling up on the couch again. "Sampling menus, trying on dresses, and listening to local bands. I didn't get to do any of this the first time around. And you know what? It's *fun*. I had no idea, the first time around, it could be so much fun. It's probably just as well, though. I would have felt sorry for myself, and I was having a hard enough time as it was, fighting morning sickness and trying to keep my dad and Jack away from each other. I was barely even . . ." But Caroline's voice trailed off. Something outside had caught her attention and now she got up and moved toward the window that overlooked the lake. "It's snowing," she said.

"Is it? So soon?" Allie said, hoisting herself up off the couch and joining her at the window. "I thought it was supposed to start later." But there it was, falling in silvery white flurries that seemed to appear out of nowhere, right where the inky darkness of the winter night ended and the yellow glow of the cabin's lights began.

"It's not sticking yet," Jax commented, coming to stand beside Allie. "But we should probably go soon anyway."

Caroline nodded. "I'm so glad it's snowing now," she said, "as opposed to tomorrow night. This way, by the wedding, everyone will have had plenty of time to dig out from it."

"That's true. But you'll still get to have a white wedding," Allie said, and as she thought about this moment in their lives, with Caroline and Jack getting remarried, and Allie and Walker awaiting the birth of their baby, she reached instinctively for her two friends, both of whom seemed to understand what she was thinking. They put their arms around her, each on either side, and the three of them stood there, silently, for several minutes, watching the snow fall gently through the night.

Chapter Five

_____

As promised, it snowed heavily during the night, and Daisy, snuggling deeper under the covers, remembered that as a child she'd loved waking up the morning after a snowstorm to find her whole world wrapped in a layer of soft, cottony whiteness. And when she pulled back her bedroom curtains at nine o'clock that morning, she was not disappointed. At least a foot of snow had fallen overnight, and it looked like the "good snow," too, the kind you could easily make a snowball with. Or a snowman . . .

An hour later, she and her dad stood in front of the cabin, surveying their handiwork.

"What do you think?" Daisy asked.

"I think he looks a little lopsided," Jack observed of their snowman.

"*He*? Who said anything about it being a 'he'?" Daisy objected, as she started to unwrap her scarf. The sky was a deep blue, and the sun was radiating off the snow with a brilliant whiteness. Already, the icicles on the cabin's eaves were dripping, and clumps of snow were falling off the branches of the great northern pines. This snow wouldn't last long; by midday, it would be turning soft and slushy in the country, and sending streams of water running through the gutters in the town.

"I thought snowmen were always men," Jack said, taking off his coat. Like Daisy, he was hot from his exertions. He watched now as she wrapped her red woolen scarf around the snowman's neck. "I'm not an expert, though," he added. "I've never actually made one of these before today."

"Dad, are you serious?" Daisy said, pausing in her work. He nodded.

"You grew up in the state of Minnesota and you've *never* made a snowman before."

"Not that I can remember."

Daisy looked at him, and he looked back at her, and something passed between them. Something that made a hard lump form in Daisy's throat. Jack Keegan's childhood was one of those things there were no words for. Daisy didn't know a lot about it. Her dad didn't want her to. But she knew that his back was ridged with deep, puckered scars that his uncle's belt had left behind on it, and she knew too that if his memories of these beatings hadn't exactly driven him to drink—her dad said this was one of the many myths about alcoholism, that something specific could "make" you drink—they had, at the very least, contributed to it.

Now, though, her dad gave his head a little shake, and

gave her a little smile, as if to say, *It's not important. Not anymore. I have you and your mom now.*

But an anger had started to burn inside of Daisy, and she couldn't ignore it. "That man wouldn't even let you build a snowman?" she asked of the uncle who'd raised Jack on his farm after Jack's parents were killed in a car accident.

Jack shrugged. "He was all business. To him, that's all a farm was. A business. And snow . . . snow didn't mean anything, except, most of the time, more work for him. More work for *us.*"

"But didn't he and your aunt ever let you have any fun?" Daisy persisted. "Even at this time of year? I mean, they must have celebrated Christmas, right?"

"Wrong," Jack said, adding some more snow to the snowman's midsection. He seemed determined, suddenly, to work some kind of improvement on his slightly misshapen form.

"So there were no presents?" Daisy clarified.

"No presents," Jack said, glancing up from his work. "My uncle didn't like presents. He didn't see the need for them. And he didn't want to spend the money on them, either."

"And your aunt?" Daisy asked. She harbored, in some way, as much resentment for Jack's aunt as she did for his uncle. She hadn't beaten Jack. But she had let her husband beat him. She had literally looked the other way while he'd done it, and then said nothing afterward. A crime of complicity, Daisy knew, could be almost as egregious as the crime itself.

"My aunt . . ." Jack paused, still working on the snowman. "My aunt didn't like anything my uncle didn't like."

And that included you, didn't it? Daisy almost said, but she didn't. Instead, she said, in a little burst of anger, "Honestly, Dad, I could kill that man."

"Well, he died and saved you the trouble, Daisy."

"He died? When?"

"This fall."

"How?"

"He had a heart attack. An old friend of mine called and told me. I couldn't believe it at first. I always thought that man was too mean to die. And, of course, in my imagination, he was still the man he'd been when I'd left his house as a teenager. Still the big, strapping man. But no, my friend said. He'd gotten old. The way we'll all get old one day. He'd gotten all bent over, and frail and arthritic. Funny, though, I can't quite picture him that way."

"Did you . . . go to his funeral?"

"Oh, God no."

Of course not, she thought. What would have been the point? It was too late, by then. Too late to tell him . . . to tell him what?

"Dad, if you had seen him again, though, what would you have said to him?"

"Nothing."

"*Nothing?*" Daisy said in disbelief.

He shrugged. "There's nothing I could have said to that man that would have changed anything. Nothing he could have said to me, either."

"But weren't you angry at him, Dad? Aren't you still angry at him?"

"Yes," he said, simply. "Yes to both. But when I was

drinking, I wasn't as angry at him as you might imagine I'd be. Alcohol had an anesthetizing effect on me." Jack concentrated now on straightening the snowman's lop-sided head. "But when I stopped drinking, I *was* angry at him. Crazy angry. And I had revenge fantasies, too, same as you. What I'd say to him if I saw him. What I'd do to him. But then I realized that that anger was eating me up inside. And I realized another thing, too. I couldn't be in your life and your mom's life again if I was still that angry. I just couldn't. It wouldn't have worked. So I let go of it. Or I let go of *most* of it. As much as I could, anyway. There'll always be some left, of course. But I can't do any-thing about that."

And Daisy, at a loss for words, came around to his side of the snowman and surprised him with a hug. He hugged her back. "All right," he said, when the hug ended, "that's enough feeling sorry for me for one day. And besides," he added, going back to putting the finishing touches on the snowman, "I'm not alone in having had an unhappy childhood. Do you know what I read somewhere?"

"What?"

"That eighty-five percent of Americans consider themselves to have grown up in a dysfunctional family. *Eighty-five percent*. Think about it. That puts me in the majority of people."

Daisy said nothing. She wasn't sure if systematically beating a child qualified as dysfunctional so much as it qualified as criminal.

She watched as her dad brushed some loose snow off one of the snowman's shoulders with a proprietary air.

"There," he said, stepping back. "I've officially finished my first snowman. With a little help from you."

"A *little*? Dad, I did all the heavy lifting," Daisy objected, jokingly, and as she did so she reached down and scooped up some snow in her gloved hand.

"You contributed somewhat," he teased. "You put the scarf on."

She used both hands now to form the snow into a perfect ball, as she backed, casually, away from him. "Dad, what about snowball fights? Did you ever have one of those?"

"Yes. Those I know something about. We used to have those at school, during recess or—"

But before he could finish, she'd lobbed a snowball at him, and it had caught him on his right ear. He laughed, and he hadn't even wiped the snow out of his ear before he was reaching down and scooping up a snowball of his own to throw at her.

FIFTEEN MINUTES LATER, they came back into the cabin, knocking snow off their boots and peeling off their layers of outerwear. From the front hall, Daisy could see the Christmas tree in the living room, all done up with white lights, white ribbons, and silver ornaments. It amused Daisy that each year Caroline had a Christmas tree theme; this year it was a white and silver tree. Last year it had been all animal ornaments and colored lights. One year she had strung sand dollars with white silk ribbons and hung them all over the branches. Only the profusion of colorfully wrapped presents under the tree stayed the same from year to year.

Now, as Daisy pulled off her boots, flushed and warm from the snowball fight, she wondered why the cabin was so quiet. They'd left her mom puttering cheerfully around in the kitchen, enjoying a rare day off from Pearl's, and jotting down last-minute notes on what Daisy now referred to as her "wedding pad."

But now, as she padded into the kitchen in her slightly damp wool socks, Daisy felt a strange foreboding, and, as soon as she saw her mother, she knew she was right to feel it. She was sitting at the kitchen table, drinking coffee, a determined expression on her face. This was her mom in crisis mode, Daisy knew, and her stomach tightened immediately.

"Mom, what's wrong?"

"What's wrong?" her mom repeated, getting up and topping off her already full cup of coffee from the coffeepot on the counter.

"Mom, it's not . . . it's not anything having to do with anyone we know, is it?"

"What? Oh, no, Daisy. No, no, no," she said, pushing a strand of her strawberry-blond hair out of her face. She was still in her nightgown, and, for some reason, in the kitchen's morning light she looked incredibly young, and incredibly vulnerable, to Daisy. "It's nothing like that," she said, gesturing for Daisy to sit down at the table.

"Nothing like what?" Jack asked, coming into the kitchen.

"Nothing terrible," Caroline said, quickly. "I promise.

It's just . . . after you two went outside this morning I got a call from Lori Pell at the White Pines, and . . ."

"And?" Jack prompted her.

"There was a fire there last night. Nobody was hurt," she said quickly. "But in one of the back offices there was an electric space heater, the old-fashioned kind, with the coils in it, and someone left it on overnight. It was too close to a desk, and some papers caught fire." She paused and gulped a little more coffee. "Fortunately, it didn't reach the guest rooms, and everyone got out safely, but the main part of the inn is closed now, due to smoke and water damage. And our wedding, obviously, is canceled."

"Canceled or postponed?" Daisy clarified. "I mean, they're going to reopen, aren't they?"

"Absolutely. But it will be several weeks, if not months, before they do, so I told Lori I wanted to cancel. On the bright side, though," she said, not looking very bright, "we're getting our deposit back. Now I'm going to have to call the florist and the bakery, too. If it's too late for them to return our money, I'm going to ask them to donate the flowers, and the cake, to charity."

"Oh, Mom," Daisy said, sadly, reaching out and squeezing her hand. And Jack came around behind Caroline and put both his hands on her shoulders.

"Sweetheart," he said, "I'm so sorry."

"I know," Caroline said, a little tremulously. "I was stunned when Lori called. I felt like the floor had opened up beneath me. And I'm not going to lie. There were a few tears, too. But then I decided I was being a little melo-dramatic. Not to mention a little selfish. Our problems are nothing compared to Lori's right now. But there you have it."

"Mom, you're still having a wedding, aren't you?" Daisy asked.

"Well," she said, patting one of Jack's hands, which was still on her shoulder. "We'll still have a wedding ceremony. But I think it will be just family. And it doesn't look like there's going to be a reception."

"But you got your deposit back, Mom. Why can't you just move the wedding somewhere else?"

"You're not the first person to suggest that, Daisy. As soon as I got off the phone with Lori, Allie called, and then Jax, one after the other. Bad news travels fast in Butternut," she added, sipping her coffee. "They tried to help. Allie offered their cabin for the wedding—"

"Oh, Mom, say yes," Daisy interrupted, thinking of how gorgeous Allie and Walker's "cabin" was.

"I already said no. Allie is eight-and-a-half months pregnant. There's no way I'm putting her through the stress of hosting fifty people at a reception. After I'd gotten off the phone with her, though, Jax called. She agreed with me about Allie's cabin, but she suggested the American Legion or the Community Center."

"Both good suggestions," Daisy pointed out.

"Honey, no. The American Legion, the site of a thousand fish frys, is not going to be the site of my wedding. And, as for the Community Center, everyone knows the events room there reeks of chlorine from the pool next door."

"There's got to be someplace," Daisy murmured, thinking.

"On this short notice? That's doubtful. But even if there were someplace, Daisy, it misses the point."

"Which is?"

"Which is that after the initial shock and disappointment, somewhere between the time I hung up with Lori and the time the two of you came back inside, I realized that I'd gotten off track. I'd lost sight of what was important. And it's not the dress, or the shoes, or the guest list. And it's definitely not whether I have white roses or white gardenias in my bouquet, or whether we serve beef Wellington or prime rib at the reception. What's important is our family," she said, looking from one of them to the other. "*That's* who this wedding is for. And you two are the only people I need to be there."

Daisy started to interject something here, but Caroline rushed on. "And to that end, I made a phone call myself this morning. I called Judge Hilliard." Peter Hilliard was a former Duluth Superior Court judge who, since retiring to Butternut ten years ago, had never missed a breakfast at Pearl's. Caroline had asked him, weeks ago, if he'd officiate at their wedding at the White Pines, and he'd been happy to oblige. "I told him about canceling the reception," Caroline said now, "and I asked him if we could do it privately, and do you know what he suggested? He said why didn't we come over to their house the day after tomorrow, on Christmas Eve, at around five o'clock in the evening? He said that his wife, Mary Beth, can be the second witness to our marriage, along with Daisy, and that we'll leave early enough for them to have their Christmas Eve dinner and for us to come back here and have ours. It'll have to be something simple, but it'll still be nice. Maybe I'll make a roast." She reached for her "wedding pad" on the table, and then she caught herself and shook her head a little sadly.

"I guess I won't be needing this anymore," Caroline said, picking up the pad and carrying it over to the garbage can. She dropped it in, and brushed her hands together, as if glad to be done with it. But the expression in her face was wistful. "Now, if you'll excuse me," she said, "it's about time I got dressed and started calling the guests," and she left Daisy and Jack alone in the kitchen, staring helplessly after her.

Chapter Six

THE NEXT DAY, the day that was *supposed* to have been Jack and Caroline's wedding, Walker Ford was sitting in his office at the Butternut Boatyard. He was leaning back in his swivel chair, his work boots propped on his desk, staring at the incoming call on his cell phone's display. It was his brother, Reid, and this was the third time he'd called today. The last two times, though, Walker had let it go to voice mail. Now he sighed, resignedly, and punched Talk.

"What?" he said, by way of a greeting.

"Well, hello to you, too," Reid said. "I'm glad I caught you in such a good mood."

"I'm not in a bad mood," Walker said, though his voice sounded a little churlish, even to him. "I just know why you're calling me, Reid."

"Why am I calling you?"

"To tell me you're not coming for Christmas."

The silence on the other end of the line confirmed this,

but then Reid said, a little defensively, "And why is that a problem, Walk? I mean, lately we can't even have a telephone conversation with each other without getting in an argument. Why would you think us seeing each other in person, over the holidays no less, was a good idea?"

"Because . . . because you're my brother," Walker said simply. And, for once, Reid was silent. He had no ready reply for this. He was, of course, Walker's brother, but at one time, he'd been so much *more* than Walker's brother, and they both knew it. When they were growing up, against the backdrop of their parents' disastrous marriage, Reid had been not just an older brother to Walker, but a protector, a mentor, a sounding board, a coach, a tutor, and last and most important, a best friend. For a long time, they'd been as close as two brothers could be, particularly during the early years of building their boatyard business together, a business that now totaled more than a dozen boatyards in three midwestern states.

But sometime after Walker had met Allie and married her, and adopted her son, Wyatt, they'd begun to drift apart. Walker's life had changed—once an inveterate workaholic and commitment-phobe, he was going out on "date nights" with his wife, coaching Wyatt's youth basketball team, and curling up on the couch with the two of them for family movie nights—and Reid's life, well, Reid's life had not changed. Reid's life had stayed *exactly* the same. Work and women, in that order, and the work part of the equation was brutal. It was not unusual for Reid to work, by choice, up to sixteen hours a day. And the women part of the equation? Well, Walker couldn't really say. Reid never dated anyone he met long enough to actually introduce her to his brother and his sister in-law.

"Look," Reid said now, his voice uncharacteristically gentle, "you know, first and foremost, that you're my brother. You'll always come first in my life. But this whole holiday thing, it's not for me. *Any* day, *any* time, *any* place you want me to grab a cup of coffee with you, or a beer, or a steak, I'll be there, you know that. Hell, I'll even go fishing with you," and Walker almost smiled, because that was saying *a lot*. Despite their shared love of boats, Reid had never shared Walker's love of fishing. The point of being out on the water, Reid had always argued, was to go fast. Reid loved going fast, on land and water, and on land, anyway, he had the speeding tickets to prove it.

"Walker, I swear," he continued, "I'll do *anything* else with you, and your family, but I won't do the whole holiday thing. The whole tree-trimming, carol-singing, present-opening thing. I'm sorry, but what can I say? Our childhood basically ruined the entire institution of Christmas for me." And Walker, listening to him, flashed on an image of their parents screaming hysterically at each other one Christmas morning, while he and Reid looked on in dismay, and the shiny new presents spread out around them rapidly lost their appeal.

"Trust me, Walker," Reid said, "it's better for all of you if I go and drown my sorrows elsewhere."

"Hmmm," Walker said, skeptically. "What's elsewhere's name?"

"What?"

"What's the name of the woman you'll be spending Christmas with?"

"Oh. Brandi. Brandi with an *i*."

"Of course it's with an *i*."

"No need to be snooty," Reid objected.

"Where'd you meet her?"

"At the gym."

Walker sighed and rubbed his eyes.

"Again with the snootiness," Reid said. "There's nothing wrong with meeting someone at a gym. I mean, it's probably better than meeting a woman at a bar. You'd be amazed, Walker, how much you can learn about someone just from working out next to her."

Walker didn't answer. He was still rubbing his eyes.

"Anyway, Brandi and I are leaving Christmas Eve to fly to Miami. I've booked a hotel suite with a private deck, because Brandi wants to sunbathe topless, and I want to . . . well, I want to *watch* Brandi sunbathe topless. And trust me, Walker, she is *so* worth watching."

"And that's it? That's how you're going to celebrate Christmas?"

"Well, the room comes with a Jacuzzi, too. And a full bar."

Walker's irritation turned, unexpectedly, to sadness. "Reid, when was the exact moment that you became a cliché?" he asked his brother. "Seriously, I'd like to know, because I think I somehow missed it."

But Reid was done with this part of the conversation. "I'm going to ignore that last remark," he said blithely. "But I want you to know that I sent a box of presents today, and it included a very expensive bottle of whiskey for you, which I expect you to save and drink with me. And I sent Wyatt a Minnesota Twins jersey, and I sent something for Allie and the baby, too. How are they doing, by the way, mother and soon-to-be child?"

"They're ... they're doing all right," Walker said.

"Just all right?"

"No, they're doing fine. I'm just ... I'm just worried about them, that's all."

"Why?"

"I don't know. There's just ... there's just things that can go wrong now, at this stage of pregnancy," Walker said, feeling it again. That gnawing sense of dread that had been visiting him, lately, every once in a while.

"What are you talking about? I saw Allie last month," Reid said. "She looked amazing. And she said the baby was kicking up a storm. They both seemed fine. Better than fine."

"As far as we know, they are both fine. It's what we *don't* know, what we *can't* know, that's worrying me. I mean, there's all this stuff that can happen in the third trimester, Reid. Things I'd never even heard of before. And it happens all the time. In perfectly normal pregnancies. Preeclampsia, for one thing," he said, hating the very sound of the word.

"What's that?"

"It's something that can lead to seizures, and kidney failure, and ..." He stopped. It was too terrible to say out loud.

"And what?" Reid prompted.

He sighed, rubbed his eyes again, and lowered his voice, almost to a whisper. "And, very rarely, it can lead to death. Of the mother and baby."

"Walker, I think *very rarely* are the key words there. Besides, it's the twenty-first century, and we're living in a developed country. There's a test for something like that, isn't there? For preeclampsia? And when it does happen, there must be a treatment for it, too."

"But, Reid, that's not the only thing that can go wrong. There's also something called—"

"Okay, *stop*," Reid commanded. "Just . . . stop. This sounds crazy. Walk, this isn't like you. Where are you even getting all this information?"

"Off the Internet," Walker admitted. "When I can't sleep at night, I . . ." His voice trailed off.

"When you can't sleep, you go online and find things that are guaranteed to scare the *hell* out of you, is that it, Walk? Jesus, I hope you're not sharing any of this with Allie."

"No, of course not."

"Well, there's that, anyway. But in the meantime, isn't there something more relaxing you can research on the Internet? Like when the next global pandemic will take place? Or how soon terrorists will be able to make a nuclear bomb?"

Walker didn't answer.

"Okay, look. Here's my advice to you. Stay away from your computer, especially in the middle of the night. Or if you can't stay away from it, use it to go to one of those fly-fishing websites you order all your lures from. Because too much information, in this case, is not a good thing." And when Walker still said nothing, Reid added, quietly, "Besides, we both know what this is about."

Walker tensed. "Do not bring that up, Reid. I mean it." *Do not bring up Caitlin's miscarriage.*

"All right, I won't," Reid said. "Just remember, there's a ninety-nine point nine percent chance that everything's going to be okay. And I know that without having to do any Internet research."

"Yeah, okay," Walker said, without any real conviction. But at that moment, he caught site of Allie standing in the open doorway to his office. She smiled, tentatively, and held up a tin of Christmas cookies.

"Allie," he said, with a mixture of both surprise and disapproval. She'd promised him she'd stay at home today and take it easy.

"Reid, I gotta go," he said, taking his feet off the desk and standing up. "I'll talk to you soon."

"Sure, and remember what I said."

"Right," Walker said, ending the call and starting to clear papers off the other chair in his office. But Allie waved him back down and came and sat on the edge of his desk instead.

"How's Reid?" Allie asked.

"Fine," Walker said, in a clipped tone.

"He's not coming, is he? But we already knew that, didn't we?"

"I guess we did. The thought of him spending Christmas with Brandi, though, is so depressing."

"Brandy, as in a bottle of it?"

"No, *Brandi* as in a *woman* named Brandi. Brandi with an *i.*"

"Well, that sounds like Reid. The *brandy* and the *Brandi*," she added, trying to get Walker to smile. But when he wouldn't smile, she said, "I know how much you wanted him to come. But he's not comfortable in family settings. He may *never* be comfortable in family settings."

"I know. You're right," he said, with a sigh. "It still doesn't stop me from trying every year, though, does it?"

"No, it doesn't. But only because you're such a good brother." And then, brightening, she said, "I brought you something." She held out the cookie tin, but when he took it, distractedly, she frowned and said, "This isn't just about Reid. You're mad at me, too."

"I'm not *mad* at you. I just thought you were staying at home today."

"I was. But I took Wyatt over to play with Jade, and then Jax and I started talking about Caroline, and about the wedding that didn't happen today."

"How's she doing?"

"Okay. I talked to her this morning, and she was her usual stoic self. Honestly, though, I think she's much more disappointed than she's willing to admit. She keeps saying that the marriage is what's important, not the wedding, but Jax and I think that's because she put her heart into the White Pines wedding, and now she can't imagine it being anything else. But Jax and I can imagine something else, and we have an idea. I mean, we're going to have to run it by Jack and Daisy first. But it could work. It could *really* work. You don't mind if we don't have our Christmas Eve dinner at home, do you?"

"No. Not if you and Wyatt and I are together," he said.

"Good." She smiled at him and then popped open the lid of the cookie tin and selected a cookie from it. "Look," she said, holding it out to him. "Jenna decorated this one especially for us." Walker looked at the cookie. It was shaped like a snowflake, and it had at least a half inch of pale blue frosting on it, and it was sprinkled with an almost insane number of tiny silver balls.

Walker looked at it doubtfully. "Is it edible?"

"Of course it's edible," Allie said, taking a bite. "It's delicious." She handed it back to Walker and he took a bite, too. But he couldn't really taste it. He was still upset about Allie driving today. He handed the cookie back to her.

Allie sighed. "All right, what is this about?"

"It's about you gallivanting around town today, when we both agreed—"

"*Gallivanting?* Walker, I stopped by a friend's house. I hardly think that qualifies as 'gallivanting.'"

He shrugged, noncommittally.

"Walker, for the one-hundredth time, I'm pregnant. I'm not an invalid."

"I didn't say you were an invalid."

"But you'd prefer I stay at home?"

"Not forever. Just until the baby's born. I mean, I know you think I'm being overly protective, but the roads can be slippery this time of year, and the sidewalks can be too."

Allie didn't say anything. Instead, she popped the rest of the Christmas cookie into his mouth, and then she slid off the desk and sat down on his lap. It wasn't as easy as it had been eight and a half months ago, but she still fit, and when she snuggled closer to him and he put his arms around her, it felt as right as it ever had.

Walker finished the cookie, and she rested her head on his shoulder, and they stayed that way for a little while until he said, "Look, I know, rationally, that you and the baby are okay, but on some other level, I can't help it, Allie. I'm scared. I'm scared for you, I'm scared for the baby, and, selfishly, I guess, I'm scared for myself, too. Scared of . . ." But again, he couldn't say it. Couldn't say "losing you," or "losing the baby." It made the possibility of either of these things seem too real.

"Walker," she said, taking her head off his shoulder and looking into his eyes. "Everything is fine. You've seen all the test results. The baby and I are both perfectly healthy."

"The tests can't test for everything," he pointed out.

"No, they can't. But intuition counts for something, too. And I just feel . . . no, I just *know*, that everything is going to be okay. You have to trust me on this one. Because that feeling reassures me more than any test ever could."

He nodded, slightly mollified, and she smiled at him and snuggled closer. *God, she was so beautiful right now,* he thought, reaching out a finger to stroke her smooth cheek. And he had to admit that as much as he'd worried about her being pregnant, he'd still loved the way she looked pregnant. He'd loved the extra sheen in her honey-colored hair, the extra brightness in her hazel eyes, and the extra glow in her pale, gold skin. He put his hand on her belly now and left it there, comforted that even through the thick wool of her maternity sweater he could feel the reassuring warmth and solidity. He stroked her belly then, gently, in a way he knew Allie liked, until he felt something jump, almost violently, under his hand. He pulled his hand away, startled, and Allie laughed. "That was quite a kick," she said. "The baby's been doing that a lot today."

He put his hand, gingerly, back onto her belly. "Remember when the kicks used to be these little fluttery things?" he asked her. "It almost felt like you had butterflies trapped in there."

"Well, not anymore," Allie said, nuzzling her cheek against his. "Our baby's getting stronger. It's getting ready to be born."

"It's amazing, isn't it?" he said, rubbing her belly again. "Even after all the books I've read, and all the programs we watched about pregnancy, and labor and delivery, the baby still doesn't seem quite real to me. He, or she, still feels like a stranger to me. Maybe that's one of the reasons I worry about it as much as I do. I don't really know who the baby is yet."

Allie looked at him thoughtfully. "Would . . . would it feel more real to you, I mean, would the baby feel less like a stranger to you, if you knew its sex?"

"Well, it's too late for that, isn't it? We told the ultrasound technician we didn't want to know."

"No, *you* told the ultrasound technician you didn't want to know. After the ultrasound was over, and you left the room, I told her I *did* want to know."

He stared at her.

"I'm sorry," she said, suddenly anxious. "Don't be mad. I know we agreed beforehand we didn't want to know. But then I was sooo curious. And I was almost positive, too, that I knew the sex from looking at the ultrasound, but then I thought, 'what if I'm wrong,' what if I walk around for the next four and a half months thinking it's one sex and then it turns out to be the other and I feel so . . . disoriented."

"Well, I guess you can't help what you saw," Walker said, absorbing this new information. "Were you, uh, right about the baby?"

"I was. And I thought about telling you, too. But you seemed so set on *not* knowing that I decided to keep it to myself. Do you . . . want to know now?"

"You're damn right I do."

She smiled. "You don't want to be surprised?"

"I *will* be surprised. As soon as you tell me. Now, what'd you see in that ultrasound?"

"Actually, it was what I *didn't* see on that ultrasound."

"You mean . . . ?"

She nodded.

"There was no . . . ?"

"Nope . . . It's a girl. *She's* a girl."

"She's . . . Brooke," Walker said wonderingly. Brooke was the name they'd chosen for a girl.

"Yes, she is," Allie agreed. "And she's going to be here before you know it," she added. His hand was still resting on her belly and now she placed her hand over it in time for both of them to feel another powerful kick. Walker didn't move his hand away this time, though. He left it right where it was.

They sat like this in silence for a few minutes, both of them perfectly happy, and then Walker said, "Well, obviously, Wyatt and I are going to have teach her how to fish."

"Obviously," Allie teased. "But, honey, what if she doesn't *like* fishing?"

"I'm not even willing to consider that possibility yet," he said, pulling her closer.

Chapter Seven

"Wait, don't get out yet," Jack said. He jumped out of the pickup he'd just parked and ran around to the other side to help first Caroline and then Daisy out. "Careful in those heels," he reminded Caroline, giving her his arm for support. She was wearing the blue silk high-heeled shoes she'd had dyed to match the dress she was wearing. She'd almost left the shoes and dress behind in her closet, thinking they'd be too formal for her new, streamlined wedding. But Daisy had overruled her; they were both so pretty, she'd said, and who knew when she'd have a chance to wear them again? Besides, how was it possible, her daughter had asked her, to be overdressed for your own wedding?

Now, as they approached Judge Hilliard's front door, Caroline felt her first flicker of nervousness, and to distract herself, she concentrated on making her way up the salt-strewn front walkway instead. The judge and his wife lived in a converted farmhouse outside of town that looked especially pretty right now with the winter sun beginning to sink behind the pine trees that bordered its meadows.

"Looks like the judge's grandchildren have been visiting," Jack said, pointing to a half-finished snowman in the yard.

"Ours is better," Daisy said, under her breath, as they climbed the front steps.

Caroline smiled and hesitated only a moment before she rang the doorbell. Then, to calm herself, she turned her attention to the wreath that hung on the front door, adjusting its slightly crooked red bow and securing one of its loose pinecones. Jack, sensing her nervousness, squeezed her hand, though she saw that he wasn't doing much better. He kept tugging, restlessly, on the tie he was wearing with his button-down shirt and blazer. Jack looked handsome in his wedding clothes, she thought, but also slightly out of his depth. After all, he was a man who felt most comfortable in T-shirts, jeans, and work boots. She could count on two fingers, she realized now, the times she'd seen him in a tie, and both times had been at his weddings to Caroline.

"Ring again, Mom," Daisy said, and Caroline did. She'd always liked Judge Hilliard, she reflected. He'd been known to be a formidable judge in Duluth before he'd retired, but he was generous and kind, and he adored his grandchildren. And he'd been a close friend of Caroline's father, too, whom he'd grown up with here in Butternut. It was too bad her dad would never get to know Jack as he was now. He'd died thinking badly of him. But he would be happy that she was happy, and perhaps, today, that would have to be enough for her.

"Hello, hello, come in," the judge's wife, Mary Beth, said, as she swung open the door. She was a tall woman with shoulder-length silver hair, vivid blue eyes, and an easy smile. Jack, Caroline, and Daisy each greeted her in turn before they took off their coats and hung them on pegs in the front hall and then followed her into the living room. A fire was roaring in the fireplace there, and pine boughs were looped cheerfully around the white wooden mantel. A fat Christmas tree covered with the old-fashioned lights Caroline remembered from her childhood dominated one corner of the room. Caroline sighed with satisfaction. The room was warm and bright and lined with windows that overlooked the farm's snowy expanses.

"Would you like something to drink?" Mary Beth asked them. "We have some delicious eggnog."

"Mary Beth makes the best virgin eggnog you've ever tasted," Judge Hilliard said, coming into the room. He was a heavyset man with ruddy cheeks, and he was wearing a dark suit and a red-and-green tie for the occasion. He gave Caroline and Daisy each a warm hug and shook hands with Jack.

"I'm so glad you've decided to do this here today. And don't you look lovely," he said, turning to Caroline.

"Thank you," she murmured, her nervousness ratcheting up, but there was Jack, again, by her side, and Daisy, smiling at her encouragingly.

Now Mary Beth brought out a tray with glasses of eggnog and a plate of Christmas cookies, and they all sat down, and sipped a little eggnog and nibbled on the cookies until, after several minutes of this, and some polite chitchat, Judge Hilliard cleared his throat and signaled that it was time for the ceremony to begin. Then the five of them arranged themselves in front of the fireplace, with Jack and Caroline facing the judge and Daisy and Mary Beth standing on either side, and a little bit behind them. Beyond the judge was a row of windows, and through them Caroline saw that the last pinkness was draining from the sky, and that the wind was kicking up little swirls of snow. A log popped and then crackled in the fire, and the smell of nutmeg lingered in the air. *This is it*, Caroline thought. *This is what I've always wanted. Jack and Daisy. My family.*

Judge Hilliard buttoned his jacket. "Shall we begin?"

Jack and Caroline both nodded, and Jack released her arm long enough to tug nervously on his tie again. *Poor man*, she thought, *he probably feels as if he's being strangled.* "One moment, Judge," she said, and she reached over and unknotted Jack's tie and slipped it off him. Then she unbuttoned the first button of his shirt, and, after folding the tie neatly, deposited it into the inside pocket of his blazer. "There, *now* we can begin," she said, and Jack, both amused and grateful, leaned over and kissed her temple.

"All right. You two have expressed a desire to recite your own vows. Do you have them prepared?"

"They're right here," Daisy said—Daisy who was both

maid of honor and best man at this ceremony. She handed Jack and Caroline each a sheet of paper.

Now Judge Hilliard cleared his throat again and spoke. "Since you both asked me several weeks ago to officiate at your wedding, I've been thinking a lot about the two of you. About how you're getting a second chance, and about how rare it is in life to get one. We're not usually given an opportunity to correct a mistake, or to right a wrong from our past. Usually, the best we can do is to be honest with ourselves, to apologize when necessary, to make peace with what we've done or failed to do, and to move forward.

"I remember speaking to your father, Caroline, shortly before he died. He said he could forgive you, Jack, for leaving his daughter and granddaughter, but he wondered if you would be able to one day forgive yourself. For forgiveness is what allows us to love. And, Caroline, another woman in your place might have become bitter over the years, raising a child and running a business alone. But somehow, through all this, neither you nor Jack lost sight of the things that matter most. Both of you have been able to forgive yourselves, and each other.

"And I'm reminded of something a poet once said about love. He said that for one human being to love another is the most difficult task given to us, but that it is also the most important. And that love is the work for which all other work is merely a preparation. I think that's true. Love brings joy, yes, but it also brings hard work. And here you both are, together again, after all these years, ready to do this hard work, but also, to partake in this great joy. So it is with immense pleasure that I preside over your wedding now and wish you real happiness in the years ahead. Would you like to read your vows?" he asked.

Caroline and Jack exchanged looks, and Jack nodded to Caroline to go first. Caroline looked down at the sheet of paper and noticed it was shaking slightly. She steadied her hands and began to read. "Jack, when we said our vows to each other for the first time, twenty-one years ago, I don't think we really understood what those vows meant and how hard it would be to uphold them. We were so young. So inexperienced. But, as Judge Hilliard just said," she said, looking up briefly and smiling at the judge, "we have a second chance now. And this time, I believe in you. I believe in *us*." Now she smiled up at Jack. "I promise to love you, as my partner, best friend, companion, and coparent. I promise to support you in times of struggle, or sickness, or disappointment or loss, and to celebrate with you all your successes and triumphs. I promise to be honest with you, to trust you, and to respect your wishes and dreams. I'm dedicated to our marriage, to our daughter, Daisy"—here she looked over at Daisy, whose face was shining with happiness—"and to our common happiness. I love you."

Now Jack looked down at his paper, but, after a moment, he crumpled it up and put it in his pocket. "I already know this by heart," he explained to the four of them, and then he placed his hands on Caroline's shoulders and looked into her eyes. "Caroline, I may have gone through a long period of my life where I did not love myself, but I have never stopped loving you. Ever. In my darkest hours, knowing you were in the world kept me going. I promise, now, to support you in all things, to be your best friend and your lover, to laugh with you when you are happy and to comfort you when you are sad. I vow to be your partner in parenthood and in work. And to watch over you and care for you and to protect you for as long as we both live. I vow to be a patient and loving father to Daisy, to be a trustworthy and faithful husband to you, and to be someone who will never take you or our union for granted. I give you my whole heart. I love you."

"Caroline and Jack, why don't you exchange rings now," Judge Hilliard said. "Jack, why don't you give Caroline her ring first." Daisy handed him the small black box with the ring inside, and he slipped a gold band onto Caroline's ring finger. Then Daisy handed Caroline a similar box and she placed a ring on Jack's finger.

"Now, you may kiss the bride!" Judge Hilliard said. And as Jack took Caroline in his arms and kissed her, she felt something wet on his cheek. *Jack was crying,* she realized with surprise, just a moment before she began to cry herself.

"THAT WAS ONE of the most beautiful wedding ceremonies I've ever witnessed," Mary Beth said, with tears in her own eyes. Daisy, too, was crying, and as she hugged Jack and Caroline, she said, "A lot of children whose parents get divorced fantasize about this day, but, in most cases, it never comes. I guess I got lucky that way."

There was more hugging, and more crying, before Judge Hilliard asked Jack and Caroline to complete the marriage license by signing it. And then he signed it, and Mary Beth and Daisy signed it as witnesses.

When the signing was over, Jack looked down at his watch and then caught Caroline's eye. She nodded almost imperceptibly and said to the judge and Mary Beth, "Thank you so much for letting us get married this evening in your lovely home. It meant so much to us to be able to share this with you. But now I think we should be leaving, so you can enjoy your Christmas Eve, and I can get our roast in the oven."

Now Daisy cast a sidelong glance at Jack, who smiled back at her. He would be glad when the next half hour was over, though. He was keeping two secrets, one from Daisy and one from Caroline, and he figured that it wasn't until they were both out in the open that he could relax and enjoy himself.

A few minutes later, the three of them were back in the pickup, the heat blasting and Caroline saying, "Daisy, we just need to make a quick detour before we head back to the cabin."

Daisy looked at Jack, questioningly. "A detour? Well, I need to stop at Pearl's," Daisy said, as Jack put the truck into gear and pulled out onto the street, heading toward the bus stop.

"Why do you need to stop at Pearl's?" Caroline asked, and now it was her turn to look confused.

"I told Jessica I'd pick up her Christmas present for me," Daisy said.

"A Christmas present? Honey, it's Christmas Eve. Can't this wait?"

"Well, no. That's the point. She wants me to have it before Christmas," and then, tapping Jack on the shoulder, she said, "Dad, where are we going?"

"All right, both of you, just relax," Jack said. "I'm the driver tonight, and if I want to take a little detour, that's my prerogative."

Caroline and Daisy were silent now, Caroline excited and Daisy perplexed, but it wasn't long before Daisy said, "Dad, this is the way . . . are we going to the bus stop?"

"It's possible," Jack said. Caroline squeezed his hand, but Daisy said nothing. He could feel the tension in the backseat mounting, though. And when he turned into the highway rest stop that doubled as Butternut's bus stop, and they saw a tall figure waiting there, duffel bag slung over his shoulder, he heard Daisy draw in a sharp breath. But she made no move to get out.

"Honey," he said, turning around, "are you going to say hello to Will or not?"

"*Oh my God*," she murmured softly, and then she bolted out of the truck and went sprinting toward him. Will dropped his duffel and held out his arms to her, and she catapulted into them with such force that Jack was afraid for a moment she would knock him over. But she didn't. Will seemed instead to absorb her body into his, and the two of them stood there, hugging, and kissing, seemingly oblivious to the world around them.

"Do you think she was surprised?" Caroline asked, after a moment.

"I think so."

"You don't think they'll be out there kissing all night, do you?"

"I hope not. They'll freeze to death."

Caroline sighed contentedly. "It's nice, though, isn't it, that the four of us get to go back to the cabin now and have dinner together?"

Jack didn't say anything.

"It's just . . ."

"Just what?"

"Well, I wish maybe I hadn't been so dead set on not having a reception after the White Pines fell through. Not that I'm not happy now," she said quickly. "But it would have been nice, in a way, to share tonight with our friends, too."

"It might have been," Jack said, noncommittally, and he was careful not to smile.

Chapter Eight

"JACK, DO WE really need to stop at Pearl's now?" Caroline asked, as their pickup cruised down Main Street. Will and Daisy were cuddling in the backseat, talking quietly to each other, and Caroline was suddenly anxious to get back to the cabin. If they didn't start dinner soon, she worried, they'd be eating at midnight.

But as they crossed the next intersection, Caroline saw Pearl's coming up on the right-hand side of the street. The venetian blinds were drawn, but its lights were on, and its windows presented a cheerful square of yellow light to a mostly dark Main Street.

"Jack," she said, turning to him again, but he only smiled.

"Patience, Caroline," he said, reaching over and squeezing her knee as he angled into a parking space. And as he came around to her side to open her door, and helped her out, she could have sworn she heard music coming from Pearl's, music and voices and laughter. Jack walked up to the front door of the coffee shop then and rapped loudly on the glass, and Caroline saw one of the venetian blinds crack open for a second and then snap back into place. And the next thing she knew, the door was opening, and Allie and Jax were both standing there, both of them dressed in bright holiday dresses—and both of them were bubbling over with excitement.

"What . . . what is going on?" Caroline mumbled, but Jack was already taking her by the arm and leading her into Pearl's.

"Congratulations," Jax and Allie chimed, and as Jax pulled a stunned Caroline into a hug, she explained, "We figured surprising you was the only way you were going to have a wedding reception. I mean, no offense, Caroline, but your stubbornness is legendary."

"Amen to that," Daisy said cheerfully, as she and Will came in behind them and closed the door on the icy cold.

But Caroline was speechless, her eyes traveling around a room that only vaguely resembled the coffee shop that she spent three hundred and sixty days a year in. The lights were turned down low, and the tables that had been pushed together to form one long table down the center of the room were covered with white linen cloths, vases of white gardenias, flickering white candles, and her grandma Pearl's wedding china. This table, and the white lights lining the windows, and the gold stars hanging from the ceiling, gave the room a fairy-tale quality. Standing around the room, and beaming at her and Jack, were Allie and Jax, Walker and Wyatt, Jax's husband, Jeremy, and their four daughters, Frankie and Jessica, and even Walt Dickerson, Jack's AA sponsor and a man known for his legendary cantankerousness.

"How . . . how did you . . . ?" she said, turning to Allie.

"With a little ingenuity, and a lot of sneakiness," she said, laughing. "First, we had to call the florist and the bakery and tell them that under no circumstances were they to give your flowers and cake away. Then, we had to have Jack and Daisy smuggle your grandma Pearl's china out of your cabin—no easy feat, by the way—and then we had to enlist everyone's help." She gestured to the people standing around the room. "Frankie's roasting the turkey in your industrial oven, Jax and her daughters made the mashed potatoes, Wyatt and I made the cranberry sauce, and Lonnie Hagan, bless her heart, made the stuffing and the rolls."

For the second time that day, Caroline blinked back tears, and for a moment, the combination of the magical beauty of the room, the delicious smells of the dinner, and the feeling of being surrounded by all her favorite people on this most important of nights was almost too much for her. But then Will was helping her take her coat off, and Daisy was pressing a glass of punch into her hands, and everyone was coming up to congratulate her and Jack, and even Walt, who Caroline had long since labeled a cranky old man, was gracious and complimentary.

"You look beautiful tonight, Caroline," he said, his handlebar mustache tickling her as he kissed her lightly on the cheek. "And congratulations," he added. "You and Jack are very lucky to have found each other again."

"Thank you, Walt," she said, surprised by his new gentleness. And when he'd retreated, she turned to Jack, whose eyebrows were raised in surprise.

"Who knew he could be so charming," Jack said.

"Not me," Caroline said.

"What do you think?" Jack asked her then, surveying the warm, festive, and lively room.

"You know what I think?" Caroline said, realizing she was going to have a wedding reception after all, even if it was a wedding reception that doubled as a Christmas Eve dinner. "I think I'm glad I let Daisy talk me into wearing this dress."

Chapter Nine

"DAISY, SHOULDN'T WE go back now?" Will asked into the hollow at the base of her neck, which he was kissing lavishly. No, not kissing. Not exactly. Kissing didn't quite do justice to what it was he was doing to her neck. Because the truth was, he wanted to simultaneously kiss every single inch of her. He wanted to *inhale* her. The taste and touch and feel of her, after four months apart, was such that he simply couldn't get enough of her. *Wouldn't* get enough of her, he suspected, until they were truly alone later that night.

Now he pulled his mouth away from the pale, silky hollow of her neck and said, though he was already dreading having to leave this cramped little room, "We should go back now. They'll notice . . ."—he stopped to kiss her neck again—"they'll notice we're not there." Not long after they'd arrived at Pearl's, amid the music and the laughter the two of them had slipped out of the coffee shop's back door, and into a supply closet that was wedged between the office and the walk-in refrigerator.

"No, no, they won't notice we're gone," she said. "Not yet."

"But the turkey . . . ?"

"That turkey's huge," she murmured, her fingers skating up under his combat fatigues and running hungrily over his back. "It's going to take Frankie forever to carve it."

Will wasn't so sure. Frankie was a big man, and a twenty-five-pound turkey was hardly a match for him. But the feel of Daisy's hands on his skin temporarily clouded his judgment. He went back to kissing her neck, then changed his mind and kissed her mouth— marveling again at its almost indescribable sweetness— then changed his mind again and kissed her temple, her forehead, her cheek, any part of her that his lips could reach. And as he was doing this, Daisy ran her hands around to his chest and, palms splayed open, ran them up to his sternum, his collarbone, his shoulders.

"I like your uniform," she said.

"I like your dress." He ran a hand down its silky front. "But I also want to take it off you."

"You *better* take it off me."

"Later," he promised. "But I don't have to wear my fatigues to this dinner. There's something else in my duffel I could—"

"No, don't change. Really, it's true what they say about a man in uniform."

"What do they say?"

"I . . . I can't remember right now. But it's something good."

"I was going to wear regular clothes today, but I didn't have time to change."

"When did you know you were coming?" she asked, their bodies pressed together.

"Honestly, not until five minutes before I needed to leave for the airport."

"Why such short notice?"

"I'd put in for the leave. Called your parents. Made all the reservations. But my commanding officer didn't decide until the last minute."

"What did you tell him when you asked for the leave?"

"I told him I wanted to ask my girlfriend to marry me."

Daisy stopped breathing. He knew she did because her chest, which was touching his chest, stopped rising and falling.

"And I do, Daisy, I do want to ask you to marry me. I told myself I'd do it the first time we were alone tonight. But I didn't know the first time we'd be alone would be in a room that had mops in it."

She started to breathe again, and then to laugh, and to cry at the same time. "I love you," she said, pulling him against her. "I love you so much, Will. And I don't care if you propose to me now, just as long as you propose to me sometime, okay? Sometime in the not-too-distant future."

"I will," he said, carefully brushing her strawberry-blond hair off her now wet cheeks. "Because I want the next wedding either of us attends to be ours."

"Actually, it might be Jessica and Frankie's."

"Then the one after that," he said, kissing away a salty tear.

"You don't think . . . you don't think my mom's going to flip out about this, do you? I mean, eventually?"

"Last summer she would have. But not anymore. Daisy, she's been great. So supportive about my coming here. Your dad, too. He's getting up at six A.M. tomorrow morning to drive me to the airport in Minneapolis."

"*Six A.M.*? Will, you just got here."

"I know. I only have a forty-eight-hour leave, and I couldn't get a direct flight." He felt the sting of her disappointment, then her acceptance of it, and then a new resoluteness animating her.

"Never mind," she said, kissing him. "It doesn't matter. We'll just make the most of the time we have. And I'll drive you to the airport tomorrow."

"No, you can come, but you can't drive."

"Why not?"

"Because you're not going to be getting any sleep tonight," he said.

"You're right about that," she murmured, as he ran his hand down one of her stocking-covered legs and back up again. The feel of this silky material was a new sensation for him. Theirs had been a summer romance, a warm weather romance, and Daisy's unofficial uniform had been one of cotton sundresses, and short-sleeved T-shirts, and denim shorts. Still, he liked her stockings, he decided. He liked everything about her, no, he *loved* everything about her, and he told her that now.

She cried a little more and hugged him to her. "So you're okay, Will? Really okay?"

"I'm okay," he said. "The only time I was really less

than okay was when we'd have to go a couple of days without talking, and I'd think—I know this sounds crazy—I'd think, just for a second, what if you weren't real? What if I'd somehow imagined you?"

"Will, that *is* crazy."

"I know," he said, running his hands through her soft, sweet-smelling hair and thinking that she couldn't possibly be more real than she was right now. This would hold him, he knew, this night, at least until he could see Daisy again in two months. There was only one thing that was worrying him now. He skimmed a hand down her body again. It felt different. Thinner.

"Did you lose weight?" he asked.

"Yes. But it's okay. I've done nothing but eat since I got home, and now I'm about to have a five-thousand-calorie meal. Which reminds me . . ."

"I know. We need to go," Will said, kissing her, tenderly. "I love you, Daisy."

"I love you, Will," she said, wiping a final, latent tear off her cheek. And then they left the storage room, turning off the light behind them, and they headed back toward the sounds of the celebration. As it turned out, this was the first of many trips they made to that funny little room over the years ahead. Whenever they visited Pearl's, one or the other of them would inevitably drag the other one in there for a kiss. Because as unglamorous as the space itself was, with its mops and buckets and cleaning supplies, it had for them an almost incalculable sentimental value.

As CAROLINE AND Jack sat down at the head of the table, now practically groaning under the weight of all the food, Caroline caught sight of Daisy and Will letting themselves in through the back door of Pearl's. They looked flushed, happy, and only slightly disheveled. She suppressed a smile and looked tactfully away. *Ah, young love,* she thought fondly, though, if the truth be told, she was feeling plenty young herself tonight.

Daisy and Will slipped into their seats now, beside Caroline and Jack, and Jax herded a few of the younger children into their places at the table, too. And when they were all sitting down, Caroline leaned over and said, "Do you want to say a few words, Jack?"

Ho nodded and, a little shyly, stood up. The table fell quiet. "I'm going to try to keep this brief," he said. "Because I know people who've worked as hard as all you have worked to bring us this wonderful dinner, and who have traveled as far to be here with us tonight as Will has traveled, deserve to be fed without further delay." Here he smiled and reached for his glass of punch on the table. "So, to Christmas," he said, raising it up. "To friendship. And to love."

"To love," the room echoed, as fifteen more glasses were raised in unison.

New to the *New York Times* and *USA Today*
bestselling Butternut Lake series?
Then be sure to read Allie and Walker's story in

Up at Butternut Lake

and find Caroline, Jack, Daisy, and Will in

Butternut Summer

Available now in print and
e-book from William Morrow!

And don't miss

Moonlight on Butternut Lake

the next charming novel from
New York Times and *USA Today*
bestselling author
Mary McNear,
coming May 2015 from William
Morrow Paperbacks!
Read on for a sneak peek . . .

An excerpt from *Moonlight on Butternut Lake*

Chapter One

"Miss? *Miss?*"

Mila jerked awake, and stared, uncomprehendingly, around her. "Where are we?" she asked, and her voice sounded strange to her.

"Butternut," the bus driver said. "This is the last stop."

The last stop. That sounded ominous, she thought as her hand moved to massage her stiff neck.

"I saw you'd fallen asleep," the driver continued, almost apologetically. "But I remembered your ticket said Butternut. And I thought if you could sleep through that baby's screaming, you must really need the rest."

Mila nodded, annoyed at herself for falling asleep. That was stupid. She was going to have to learn to keep her guard up. And not just some of the time, but *all* of the time. She started to stand up, but her cramped legs rebelled. She sat back down.

"Take your time," the driver said, genially, looking every

bit the grandfather Mila imagined he must be, with his thick shock of white hair and pleasantly crinkled blue eyes. "You've been the only passenger since Two Harbors. Not many people travel this far north, I guess. Why don't you take a minute to stretch and I'll get your baggage out for you."

Mila nodded, then stood up again, slowly this time, and tested her legs. They were stiff, but otherwise functional. She gathered up her handbag, which she'd been careful to wedge between herself and the side of the bus, and made her way down the aisle.

When she climbed down the bus's steps, she saw that the driver was holding her suitcase and looking, doubtfully, around.

"Is someone meeting you here?" he asked.

"They're supposed to be," Mila said, a little uncertainly.

"Good," he said, handing her a slightly battered suitcase. "Because they don't get much traffic out this way. I don't know why they have the bus stop out at this junction, instead of right in the town."

But Mila had no opinion about this. Until six days ago, she'd never even heard of Butternut, Minnesota. Still, she had to admit, what she'd seen of it so far didn't look very promising. There was no bus station here, for instance, only a rest area, whose cracked asphalt was overrun with weeds, and whose sole amenities were an old bus shelter and a lopsided bench.

"I hope your ride comes soon," the driver said. "I hate to leave you here alone, but I've got to be getting back to the Twin Cities. My grandson's got a Little League game tonight," he added.

"Well, good luck to him," Mila said. "And thank you."

He started to get back onto the bus then, but Mila had a sudden thought. "Excuse me, sir," she said. "Can I ask you a favor?"

He stopped, halfway up the bus's steps, and turned around. "Name is Bob," he said, indicating his name tag. "And you can ask me a favor. I'll be happy to do it for you, too, if it doesn't take too long."

"It won't," she said. "I was wondering if . . ." Her voice trailed off. She had no idea how to phrase this. She thought about it and started over. "I was wondering, Bob . . . if someone was looking for me, and they tracked me down as far as, say, the bus station in Minneapolis, and they asked you if you'd seen me . . . if they, you know, described me to you, or showed you a photograph of me, could you . . ." She hesitated again. "Could you tell them you haven't seen me?"

Bob frowned. "Are you asking me to lie, miss?"

"Not lie, exactly," Mila hedged. "More like forget."

"Forget I ever saw you?"

She nodded.

Bob shifted, uncomfortably. "Are the police looking for you?" he asked. "Because if they are—"

"No," Mila said, relieved to be telling the truth. "No, I promise, it's nothing like that. I'm not a criminal. I'm just . . ." She paused again here. "I'm just someone who's trying to start over, that's all."

Bob gave her a long speculative look. "So you want a fresh start?"

"Exactly."

"And you don't want to bring any old baggage with you?" he asked, with a smile.

"None," she said, smiling back. "Except maybe this," she amended, swinging her suitcase.

"Okay, that's fair," Bob said. "If anyone asks—anyone not in a uniform, that is—I'll say that I've never laid eyes on you before."

"Thank you, Bob," Mila said, gratefully, swallowing past something hard in her throat. But she caught herself. *Don't you dare cry, Mila.* Because then he really *will* remember you. Besides, he can't start comforting you now. The man's got a Little League game to get to.

"Well, good luck," Bob said. He climbed up the rest of the steps, slid into the driver's seat, and pulled the lever that closed the bus's door.

"Thanks again," Mila called, relieved that the danger of her crying had subsided. Bob held up his hand to her in a good-bye gesture, started the engine, and eased the bus back onto the road. Mila watched him drive away, then dragged her suitcase over to the bench. She sat down on it, but no sooner had she done this than it began to rain. Not a hard rain. Just a dull, gray rain. Although it had been an unusually warm spring in Minnesota, today, the third day of June, was shaping up to be cool and wet.

So she stood up and carried her suitcase over to the bus shelter's narrow overhang, hoping to get a little protection from the rain. It was better there, but not by much. She shivered in her thin cotton blouse and skirt and wished she'd worn something warmer. But she'd tried to dress as innocuously, and as forgettably, as possible, and this was the outfit she'd settled on.

She saw something then, out of the corner of her eye, and she flinched. But when she turned to see what it was, she realized with relief that it was nothing more than a crow alighting on a nearby telephone line.

Would this ever end? she wondered. This constant looking over her shoulder? This fear, always, of being followed? Of being discovered? She had a sinking feeling that it would not. Unless the unthinkable happened. And he found her.

"REID? *REID*? ARE you listening to me?"

"Of course," he lied, though, in fairness to him, he had *tried* to listen to what his sister-in-law, Allie, was saying to him. But the painkillers—the painkillers that didn't seem to kill the pain—were making him a little foggy.

He watched now as Allie lifted her six-month-old daughter, Brooke, out of her stroller and settled her onto her lap. *Cute baby,* he thought, and, almost as if she knew what he was thinking about her, Brooke wriggled in her mother's arms and smiled at him, a toothless, charming smile. And then, for an encore, she balled up her tiny fist and shoved the entire thing into her mouth. *Very impressive,* Reid thought. Funny how he'd never known before how entertaining babies could be. Much more entertaining than adults, he decided, as he watched Brooke suck mightily on her little fist.

But apparently, while he was doing this, Allie was trying to talk to him, because now her voice intruded on him again. "Reid? Please try to stay with me, all right?" she asked. "Just for a few minutes." She sounded exasperated. Exasperated and something else. Concerned. Reid tensed warily. Because if there was anything he hated, it was being on the receiving end of concern.

"Do I sense a lecture coming on?" he asked now, finally tearing his eyes away from the baby. And his voice, even to him, sounded odd. Thick, and cottony. As if he didn't use it that much anymore. Which, of course, he didn't.

"A lecture?" Allie asked now, raising her eyebrows. "No. Not a lecture. Not exactly."

"Because that sounded to me like the beginning of a lecture," he said, reaching for the glass of ice water on the table in front of him. It was hard to reach from his wheelchair, though, especially since when he leaned too far forward, the full cast on his left leg dug into his thigh, and his mending ribs ached from the effort. Still, he reached for it, and, misjudging the glass's distance, his fingers only brushed against it, knocking it off the table.

"Damn it," he said, as the glass shattered on the floor. And, as if on cue, Brooke started to cry.

"Shhh," Allie said, trying to soothe her. "Caroline," she called out to the woman who owned the coffee shop. "We're going to need a broom and dustpan over here."

Reid reached down to pick up a piece of broken glass, but the side of his wheelchair limited his range of movement.

"Damn it," he said again, giving up.

"It doesn't matter, Reid," Allie said, reaching over to pat his hand, which was resting on the arm of his wheelchair. "It's just a glass. I'm sure it happens all the time here."

"But I scared the baby," Reid said, wondering what kind of a jerk you needed to be to scare a baby.

"Reid, she's fine," Allie said, putting the baby up on her shoulder and patting her on her back. "She's just tired, that's all. She's overdue for her nap."

Caroline appeared then with a broom and a dustpan.

"I wish I could tell you this was our first broken glass of the day," she said to Reid, sweeping up the fragments of glass. "But it's our third. And today was a slow day, too."

Reid looked away and mumbled an apology.

Caroline left with the dustpan and broom and came back with another glass of water, this one with a bendy straw in it. She handed the glass to Reid and waited until he had a firm grip on it before she let go of it.

"Thanks," Reid said, sipping from the straw.

"There you go," Caroline said, sounding pleased. But Reid felt himself sink a little farther into his wheelchair. *Is this what it's come to?* he wondered. *Holding my own glass and drinking from a bendy straw now constitutes a major accomplishment?*

"Allie," Caroline said. "Why don't I take Brooke for a little while? You and Reid are obviously trying to talk."

"*Trying* being the operative word," Allie murmured. But she smiled as she handed Brooke over to Caroline. "We just need a few minutes," she said, shifting her gaze back to Reid. *A few minutes,* Reid thought hopefully, as the sound of the baby's fussing receded into the background. Even he could handle a few minutes of being lectured to.

"Look, Reid," Allie started again, "I can only imagine how difficult it's been for you since the accident. And Walker and I have tried to be patient, and we've tried to give you time to adjust to all the changes in your life. But, Reid, sometimes we feel like we're the only ones who *are* trying."

Reid sighed wearily. So this was about his attitude. Which, admittedly, was pretty poor. But he was in a wheelchair, for Christ's sake, dependent on other people for all but his most basic of needs, and there were days, still, when the pain was so bad he was convinced the pills he took were nothing more than placebos.

"Look, I'm sorry," he muttered now. "I'll do better, okay?"

"Reid, you said that the last time we had this conversation."

"Well, I mean it this time."

Allie didn't look optimistic. "Reid, as of last week," she reminded him, "you've been through two home health aides."

"I know that," he said, still sipping from his straw. "But I can't help the fact that they were both completely incompetent."

"That's a matter of opinion," she said. "Walker and I, for instance, are of the opinion that they were both perfectly competent."

"Right. Well, maybe that's because you didn't have to live with either of them."

"Maybe," Allie conceded. "But the fact remains that both of them quit, Reid. And they both gave the same reasons for quitting, too. They said that you were condescending, rude, and uncooperative."

Reid, knowing this was a fairly accurate representation of his behavior, chose not to defend himself.

"The agency we've been using, Reid," Allie continued, "has refused to place another aide with you."

He shrugged. "No great loss there. They were clearly scraping the bottom of the barrel already."

Allie frowned, and a line appeared between her pretty hazel eyes. Reid immediately felt bad. He *liked* Allie. Most of the time, in fact, he liked her even more than he liked his brother, Walker, who, though younger than Reid, had lately developed the annoying habit of behaving like an older brother. But still, Allie didn't understand what it was like to have these people—these home health aides—living in your house. These people whom you had nothing in common with, but who were nonetheless privy to every detail of your life. He shuddered now, just thinking about the enforced intimacy he'd had to endure with the last two aides.

"Look," Allie said, pressing on, "I know how much you value your privacy. And I know having someone you don't know well living with you hasn't been easy, Reid, but it has been necessary. Because as much as we'd like to take care of you ourselves, we can't. We have Brooke and Wyatt," she said, Wyatt being their nine-year-old son. "And Walker's running the business by himself until you're ready to come back to work, and I'm heading into the busy season for the Pine Cone Gallery," she added, referring to the gallery where she'd worked for several years before buying it from the owner the previous summer.

"Allie, look, I know how busy you both are," he said. "But I don't expect either of you to babysit me. In fact, I don't *want* either of you to babysit me. Especially since I'm capable of taking care of myself. As in *all of the time*," he stressed. "Really, Allie. I'm ready to live alone again."

At this, Allie crossed her arms across her chest and leveled Reid with a *you have got to be kidding me* look.

"I'm not kidding," Reid said, to her unspoken comment. "I'm completely serious. I'll be fine on my own. And, if I need help, you and Walker are only a phone call away."

"No, absolutely not," Allie said, shaking her head. "You're not living in that cabin by yourself."

"Why not? You two had it completely retrofitted while I was in the rehabilitation center. I can use the bathroom by myself, get in and out of bed by myself—"

But here Allie interrupted him. "Look, it's great you're able to have some independence. But someone needs to be with you at all times. I'm sorry if that's hard for you to accept. But you were in a serious accident, Reid. You almost *died*. The doctor said it's going to be months— *many months*—before you fully recover."

"*If* I fully recover," Reid offered. After all, it was what they were both thinking.

"I didn't say that, Reid. And I didn't mean it, either. You *will* recover. But it's going to take time. And during that time, you're going to need help. However galling it may be to your pride."

What pride? Reid wondered, looking down at his

damaged leg. It had been a long time since he'd felt anything even remotely resembling pride.

But if he was wallowing in self-pity now, Allie chose not to see it. She had something else on her mind, Reid realized. Something else she needed, but didn't want, to say to him. He watched while she bit her lower lip, something he knew she only did when she was nervous.

"Allie, what is it?" he asked quietly. "What'd you bring me here for? I mean, other than to tell me I need to improve my attitude?"

Allie sighed. "Reid, that *is* why I brought you here. That, and to tell you that we've found another home health care aide. This one from Minneapolis."

"Minneapolis?"

She nodded. "We had to find a new agency, remember? Anyway," she said, glancing at her watch, "Walker's picking her up at the bus stop right now, and then he's bringing her here to meet us."

"Like a blind date?" Reid asked, cringing at the thought. "Is that really necessary?"

"Yes, it is, Reid. Because this time, you're going to make an effort. This time, you're going to be civil, right from the start, in the hopes that your civility will be habit forming. Because Walker and I have both agreed that if this placement doesn't work out . . ." She hesitated here. "If it doesn't work out, you're going to have to go back to the rehabilitation center."

"What?" Reid said, aghast. "Allie, you can't send me back there."

She wavered, and Reid knew how difficult this was

for her. She liked him. Even when his and Walker's relationship was at its most acrimonious, Reid and Allie had always gotten along.

"We don't *want* to send you back there," she qualified. "But we will. If you can't make in-home care work, we won't have any choice, Reid."

He shook his head, disgusted. When he'd first arrived at the rehabilitation center, after three weeks in the hospital, he'd been in too much pain to really know where he was, let alone to care. But as he'd started to improve, and to take stock of the situation, he'd come to appreciate how truly depressing the place was. Even thinking about it, he could smell the disheartening odor of disinfectant overlaid by furniture polish, and he could hear the constant drone of a roommate's television set, always tuned, somehow, to the same inane game show.

"I won't go back there," he said now.

"Then make this work," Allie said, almost pleadingly. "It's only for three months, okay? After that, hopefully, you'll be ready to live on your own again. In the meantime, just . . . just be nice to this woman. Her name is Mila. Mila Jones. And, for some reason, she wants to spend the summer two hundred and forty miles from her home in the Twin Cities. And, not only that, but she comes highly recommended from the woman who owns the agency in Minneapolis. So please, Reid. Please try."

He looked at Allie. She looked hopeful. Hopeful and trusting. But more than that, he thought, she looked tired. And it made him feel guilty. Paired with the arrival of a new baby, his accident, he knew, had been a lot for Allie and Walker to handle. Not that they ever complained about it. They didn't. They left the complaining to him.

"All right, I'll try," he said finally, forcing himself to smile one of his increasingly rare smiles. "This time, I'll really try."

About the Author

New York Times and *USA Today* bestselling author Mary McNear is a writer living in San Francisco with her husband, two teenage children, and a high-strung, minuscule white dog named Macaroon. She writes her novels in a local donut shop, where she sips Diet Pepsi, observes the hubbub of neighborhood life, and tries to resist the constant temptation of freshly made donuts. She bases her novels on a lifetime of summers spent in a small town on a lake in the northern Midwest.

Discover great authors, exclusive offers, and more at hc.com.